Ple£
avoi

Fenella-Jane Miller lives in an ancient cottage in acres of Essex woodland near Colchester with her husband. She worked as a teacher, restaurateur and hotelier before becoming a full-time writer.

THE UNCONVENTIONAL MISS WALTERS

Eleanor Walters is obliged, by the terms of her aunt's will, to marry a man she dislikes: the irascible, but attractive, Lord Leo Upminster . . . Leo finds Eleanor's unconventional behaviour infuriating, her beauty irresistible and their agreement not to consummate the union increasingly impossible. It is only when he allows his frustration and jealousy to drive her away that he realizes what he has lost . . . Meanwhile, in her self-imposed exile on a neglected country estate, Eleanor becomes embroiled in riots and treachery. In a desperate race, can Leo save both her life and their marriage?

FENELLA-JANE MILLER

◆

THE UNCONVENTIONAL MISS WALTERS

Complete and Unabridged

ULVERSCROFT
Leicester

First published in Great Britain in 2005 by
Robert Hale Limited
London

First Large Print Edition
published 2006
by arrangement with
Robert Hale Limited
London

British Library CIP Data

Miller, Fenella-Jane
    The unconventional Miss Walters.—Large print
ed.—Ulverscroft large print series: historical romance
1. Great Britain—History—George III, *1760 – 1820*
—Fiction 2. Love stories 3. Large type books
I. Title
823.9′2 [F]

    ISBN 1–84617–442–2

Published by
F. A. Thorpe (Publishing)
Anstey, Leicestershire
Set by Words & Graphics Ltd.
Anstey, Leicestershire
Printed and bound in Great Britain by
T. J. International Ltd., Padstow, Cornwall

For Dusty,
life partner and
best friend

Prologue

1812

'Good heavens, Miss Ellie, look at the state of you! You can't go downstairs looking like that.'

'I had no intention of doing so, Mary, for that is the very reason I am here.' She could hardly stand still, her excitement making her giddy. 'Oh do hurry, Mary,' she complained, as her maid slipped an unfussy, pale-green muslin over her head. 'I have not seen Cousin Leo for months and I so want to hear about the progress of the war.'

'There, that will do, miss.' Mary stood back to admire her young charge. Eleanor's thick, wavy brown hair was, for once, carefully constrained in a plait woven around her head. There were no longer dirty smudges marring her pale oval face and the dress, although plain, was eminently suitable for a 16-year-old who was not fully out.

Eleanor spun round, her large green eyes sparkling with anticipation. 'Can I go now?'

'Yes, love, but remember not to race down the stairs. And do try and behave like a lady.'

Miss Eleanor Walters walked gracefully across the room determined not to arrive in the drawing-room in her usual pell-mell fashion. Colonel, Lord Leo Upminster, her Aunt Prudence's only godson, would raise his aristocratic eyebrows and say something decidedly horrid if she did.

Eleanor paused outside the half-opened drawing-room door to ensure her skirts were smooth and her hair still tidy. As she raised her hand to push open the door, Leo's commanding voice could be clearly heard.

'Good God, Aunt Pru, are you mad? If I wished to take a wife the last person I would choose would be Eleanor.'

She froze; she had not intended to eavesdrop but Leo's words had cut her to the quick. She had to hear what else he was going to say. Unfortunately the murmur of her aunt's reply was not clear enough to follow but the clarion, parade-ground tones of Lord Upminster's response most certainly was.

'That may very well be true, Aunt. However, a beanpole with her head in a book, and hardly a word to say for herself, would not make a suitable bride for me or anyone else.'

Eleanor did not stay to listen to the end of the conversation. Distraught, she turned and fled, her eyes wet. 'I will never forgive him, never,' she cried, as she burst back into her chamber.

'Now whatever is the matter, Miss Ellie?' Mary rushed forward to embrace her.

'Oh, Mary, he said the most awful things about me. I thought Cousin Leo liked me, I did not realize he thought I was such an antidote.'

'Calm down, Miss Ellie, and tell me what has happened.'

Eleanor sniffed inelegantly and wiped her eyes, and nose, on her sleeve. 'I did not mean to eavesdrop. I was checking my appearance before entering and I overheard him.'

Mary patted her arm encouragingly. 'Go on, tell me, what did you hear?'

'He said that I was a beanpole, a bluestocking and had nothing of value to say. He said he would not marry me as I was unsuitable and boring.'

Mary was at a loss to know how to reply to such an astounding piece of news. 'Perhaps it was not quite as you heard it, miss; they could have been talking about someone else, not you at all.'

Eleanor's chagrin was rapidly being replaced by indignation. 'He most certainly was, Mary; I heard him use my name. He is the rudest, most uncivil, arrogant man I have ever met.' The fact that he was the only unattached man she was acquainted with appeared to escape her attention. 'I would not marry him now, if he was the last man alive in Christendom.'

'Then that is all right. If he has no wish to marry you and you do not wish to marry him, I cannot see what all the palaver is about, Miss Ellie.'

Eleanor walked over to stare out of the window. For once the magnificent view across the open park, and the green of the distant woodland, failed to soothe her. There was something about the conversation she had overheard that eluded her; suddenly she realized what it had been.

'Good grief, Mary, Aunt Prudence must have asked him to offer for me. Why else would they have been discussing a possible union between us?' Her question was rhetorical. 'How dreadful! How mortifying. How could she? I will never be able to look him in the face again without embarrassment.' Her mind made up she turned back to Mary, waiting expectantly, for the next outburst. 'Quickly, Mary, help me undress.'

'Undress, miss, whatever for?' Mary was quite bewildered by this strange request.

'If I pretend that I am unwell, unable to go down, then I shall not be obliged to face him.'

'But what if he stays for a week? You

can hardly stay in bed for so long; her ladyship would send for the doctor and you would be discovered.'

'He never stays for more than a night so I am sure he will depart tomorrow. Now hurry, for I wish to be in bed before someone is sent up to fetch me.'

'Whatever shall I say is ailing you? You were galloping all over the park on that horrid horse of yours before breakfast; you were obviously fit as a flea then, weren't you?'

Eleanor fell back, dramatically, against her pillows and covered her eyes. 'Oh Mary,' she moaned most realistically, 'I have the most awful megrim. Please shut the curtains, and fetch me a tisane to ease the pain.'

For a moment Mary was concerned. 'Good gracious, I almost believed you were ill, it gave me quite a turn, miss.'

Eleanor giggled. 'You see, Mary, if I can deceive you I shall have no trouble with Aunt Prudence. Now, draw the curtains please, for we must make my sickroom look authentic.' Eleanor's deception was consummately done and she was left to recover from her sick headache in peace.

When Lord Upminster departed, the following morning, he was unaware that Eleanor had overheard his apparently unkind words. If she had remained longer outside the room she would have realized her error. Leo had spoken in jest and had been firmly taken to task by his aunt Prudence.

'Come, do not jest, Leo. Ellie is at an awkward age; she will be an accomplished and lovely young woman when she is full grown.'

Leo grinned. 'I am sure she will. However, I have no desire, at the present, to become leg-shackled and Ellie is still far too young.'

'But you are not refusing to consider it, are you, my boy?'

'No, aunt, I am not.' He glanced towards the door. 'As Ellie is joining us, I suggest we let the matter rest.'

But Eleanor did not come down; she remained in her room and her antipathy to Lord Upminster had several years to fester, unchallenged.

1

1815

'Listen to me, miss! You have no choice, you will marry me.' Lord Upminster, was unable to comprehend that he had been roundly refused by the ill-mannered chit standing calmly before him. Eleanor's cool detachment and apparent disdain only added fuel to his fury. She smiled slightly, hoping to keep intact the polite façade but her hands were trembling so hard she was afraid they would reveal her fear. Leo regained control of his temper. He was, as a colonel in the Light Infantry, used to having his commands obeyed, instantly, and Eleanor's refusal had so surprised him that for a moment his iron control had deserted him.

'I am sorry I raised my voice. It was unpardonable, barrack-room manners, I am afraid.' He smiled warmly hoping to win her forgiveness.

'That is quite all right, Lord Upminster, pray do not mention it again. But I am sorry, my answer must remain the same. I have no wish to marry, not you or anyone else.'

The soldier shook his head in disbelief. 'Let me run through your situation once more, my dear.' His tone was avuncular, as though talking to a child. 'As you know on Aunt Prudence's sad demise, you became my ward and will remain thus until you marry, or attain your majority.'

Eleanor nodded her agreement. 'If I am now your ward and in your control already why do I have to become your wife?'

'Aunt Prudence has left her fortune, and Monk's Hall, to me on the understanding that I marry you. She has made you my ward to ensure I do not allow you to undertake any harebrained schemes, such as becoming a governess. Do you follow me so far?'

Eleanor was forced to bow her head in order to hide a smile. Did he think she was a complete nincompoop? Of course she realized how difficult the extraordinary will made life for both of them.

Leo continued, frowning, his expression fierce, his grey eyes dark as they fixed themselves firmly on the girl supposedly sitting demurely in front of him. She had not hidden her amusement as well as she had hoped.

'The war is over; Boney's safe on St Helena and I am out of a job. The half-pay of a colonel in peacetime is not sufficient and being the second son of a duke does not, in my case, make me wealthy.'

Believing he required an answer, Eleanor said politely, 'Indeed it does not, my lord.'

He glared, daring her to interrupt again. 'You have no money of your own and no home apart from here, and neither do I. You must understand that unless we marry, at once, all the money and the house will go to Aunt Prudence's nephew Jasper Walters. Do you want this beautiful place to fall into that dissolute scoundrel's hands?'

Unwilling to risk that basilisk stare again Eleanor merely nodded, although she was eager to point out to Leo that it was not her fault that she was an orphan without visible means of support.

'Good, we are moving forward it seems.' He ran his hands distractedly through his thick black hair, at a loss to comprehend Eleanor's objection to the marriage. He had completely forgotten his unkind words spoken without a thought three years before. Eleanor, however, had still not forgiven him.

'May I say something, Lord Upminster?'

'Of course you can. What is it?'

His brusque manner did not encourage Eleanor to think he would listen with any degree of equanimity to her words. 'I do understand your position. Unless we marry

9

we will both be homeless, and in my case completely penniless, although, I must admit that I fail to comprehend why Aunt Prudence should have written such a will in the first place.' She paused, her face sad, as she remembered the last time she had spoken to her beloved aunt, just before she died.

★ ★ ★

It had been on board the ship returning them from a year-long stay in India that Aunt Prudence had fallen ill. Very soon it had become apparent that she was not going to recover; that the fever was to prove fatal.

At that time Lady Dunston had held her hand weakly, in her own hot, dry clasp. 'Ellie, darling, promise me something?'

'Anything, Aunt Prudence, I would do anything you ask. What do you wish me to do?'

Her aunt's voice was becoming weaker by the second. 'I have left you well provided for, although it might not appear so at first, but I know what I have arranged will be for the best. Ellie . . . ' The rest of her instructions were lost as, with a quiet sigh, Aunt Prudence breathed her last.

If only Eleanor had known what was planned she might have been able to dissuade her. She returned to the present with a start. She had no alternative. Leo, as her guardian, had already forbidden her to even consider seeking employment as a governess. She would have to marry him knowing he had as little wish for the union as she did. All the dreams she had long cherished of marrying only for love must now be abandoned. She had no choice; Aunt Prudence had made sure that the man she had vowed never to marry, under any circumstances, was now to be her husband.

She glanced nervously at the enormous, battle-hardened man trying hard not to glower at her, as he paced up and down the centre of the drawing-room.

'I can see, my lord, that I might have been a little hasty.' She rose elegantly to her feet and waved her hand at him, in what was a gesture of reconciliation. Leo halted, raised an aristocratic eyebrow and gave an ironic bow.

'That is, of course, perfectly possible,' he said drily. 'Are we friends again, Ellie?' Leo used her pet name deliberately.

She glanced across at Upminster, leaning against the mantel, one elegant leg resting on the fender, his cool grey eyes examining the toe of his boot. Undeniably a handsome man, but rather too uncompromising in his stance to be considered an eligible *parti*, she decided.

Outwardly, he was the picture of relaxation and sympathy, but Eleanor knew different. She could sense the hidden tension and his implacable will; she could not withstand this man and, all things considered, would marriage, even one of necessity not love, be so very awful?

'I will marry you, but it must be on my terms.' Eleanor spoke quite clearly, her words giving no indication of the erratic beating of her pulse.

Leo straightened. His eyes glittered with satisfaction and he smiled a smile of devastating charm. 'I am honoured, my dear; you have made me the happiest of men. Now what are these terms of yours?'

'I wish the marriage to remain in name only. It is, after all, a union of convenience to allow us both to have a modicum of comfort and a roof over our heads.'

'Agreed. A marriage of convenience will suit me admirably.' He paused, his eyes glittering in the firelight. 'But, of course, at some stage I will wish to set up my nursery. I want that to be clearly understood, Eleanor.'

She had no choice. 'Yes, yes; that will be acceptable.' Unbearably flustered, she stepped back, turned and sped in undignified haste from the room, her normal composure quite deserting her.

2

'Mary, you are to congratulate me,' Eleanor said, as she entered her bedchamber. 'I have been forced to agree to the marriage. It would have been senseless to continue to refuse.'

Mary beamed. 'I am sure you have done the right thing, Miss Ellie. His lordship is a fine figure of a man and with Lady Dunston's fortune at his disposal will be very plump in the pocket.'

Eleanor sighed. 'But if he had been given a choice he would never have chosen me, you know that, as well as I do. He considers me too tall, too plain and too bookish.'

'Now, miss, I am sure he does not. Why, just look at you, you are as pretty as a picture.'

Eleanor went over to the glass and stared critically at her reflection. 'I am very tall.' Then she smiled. 'But he is several inches taller so perhaps that is not a drawback.' She continued her scrutiny. 'However, my bosom is rather small and my hair too thick, too dark and too heavy. To be fashionable one must be a petite, blue-eyed blonde and I fail to qualify on any of those points.'

'You should be ashamed of yourself, fishing for compliments like that,' Mary said, her position as both friend as well as personal maid, allowing her to speak freely. 'You are a lovely young woman and well you know it. And his lordship would have to be blind if he did not see that.'

Eleanor smiled. 'I have to admit I am greatly improved from the lanky beanpole I was last time he saw me.' She giggled as something else occurred to her. 'And I do not think Lord Upminster would now consider that I had little to say for myself. I would hazard a guess that he believes I speak rather too much. Was that the luncheon gong, Mary? I suppose I had better change, I have mud all over the hem of this gown from my walk this morning.'

Mary helped her young mistress into a gown of blue dimity, with dainty silk roses around the modestly scooped neckline and a single flounce on the hem. 'It is a good thing that Lady Dunston insisted mourning dress was not to be worn. Black would be unflattering, especially on someone as pale-complexioned as you.'

'Although we are not officially mourning I think the wedding ceremony cannot decently take place for another six months. That will, at least, give me time to become better acquainted with my affianced before I am obliged to marry him.'

'And you have a trousseau to prepare, my love,' Mary told her. 'No bride can contemplate matrimony before that is finished. Go on, Miss Ellie, you are going to be late.'

Eleanor swept downstairs certain she looked her best. The three years she had spent travelling the globe with her intrepid aunt had given her the confidence and poise she had lacked as a 16-year-old. Lady Dunston had fielded, and rejected, several advantageous offers during their peregrinations. Why was it only with Lord Leo that she felt so gauche and ungainly?

Luncheon was served in the small dining-room. A cold collation had been laid out for them on the sideboard. A reflection of the green silk damask wallpaper shimmered on the surface of the polished table making it ripple like water.

Eleanor deliberately avoided the seat opposite the gilt pier-glass; she had no wish to eat her meal with a double view of his lordship. A waiting footman pulled out her chair, and she sat, placing her hands demurely in her lap.

Lord Upminster, in smart fawn breeches, polished Hessians and plain dark cloth coat looked every inch the country gentlemen. In spite of being in one of her favourite gowns Eleanor felt rather like a hedge sparrow shut in with an eagle. Leo took the chair closest to her own. The footman served them and was dismissed.

Once they were private, Leo spoke. 'I hope two o'clock will be convenient for you, my dear?'

'I beg your pardon, my lord, I was wool gathering. Would two o'clock be convenient for what?'

'For the marriage service, of course; what else could I have meant?'

Marriage service? For a second she thought she must have misheard him. Had he taken leave of his senses? Too shocked to consider before she spoke, her words tumbled out.

'Are you mad? Do you expect me to marry you after a betrothal of precisely two hours? God forbid such a thing!' She pushed back her chair so violently it crashed to the floor. 'That I have to marry you at all is the outside of enough, but to be expected to marry in such haste is unseemly, why — '

'Enough!' he barked. 'I will not be spoken to like that. You will do as you are bid, young lady, or I will not be answerable for my actions.' He towered over her, his face set, his eyes icy. She noticed his fists were clenched as though he was having difficulty restraining himself from physically chastizing her.

'I will not marry you, not now. I do not care if we both are ruined,' she cried, and so saying spun round and fled from the room for the second time that day.

Upstairs, Eleanor was still incandescent with indignation. She scrambled hastily into her blue velvet riding habit, determined to put herself as far from the loathsome Lord Leo as she could. A gallop on her chestnut stallion, Rufus, would do just that.

All Mary's entreaties failed to placate her. She would not be shouted at and treated like a child. A sharp knock at the door halted her.

'Mary, I will not see him. Do not open the door; tell him I am too upset to come.' The knock was repeated more firmly. 'Oh God — please just delay him — give me time to escape. Please, Mary, I beg you.'

'Very well, but I don't think it is wise gallivanting off like this.' But Mary could see how distressed Eleanor was and reluctantly decided to help. 'Go down the back stairs, quick now, before he comes in.'

Eleanor smiled her thanks and slipped into the adjoining dressing-room and out through the servant's door. Mary hurried across and opened the bedroom door a fraction.

Brown, the elderly butler, stood stiffly

outside. 'His lordship requests that Miss Eleanor join him in the dining-room right away.'

'Miss Eleanor is too upset to come down. Please convey her apologies to Lord Upminster,' Mary replied, and shut the door firmly in his face. What his lordship's reaction to the news would be she shuddered to think. She did not have long to wait before she found out.

Leo marched into the room without stopping to knock. 'How the hell can I apologize if you will not come — ' He stopped suddenly, aware he was talking solely to the maid. With an ominous frown he demanded, 'Well, where is she?'

'Gone for a ride, your lordship. She said she needed to clear her head,' Mary replied nervously, bobbing a curtsy. Without another word he turned and, taking the stairs two at a time, headed for the stables.

Meanwhile Eleanor had already reached the stable yard, and with the help of a stable boy was placing the saddle upon the back of her horse. Rufus was stamping his hoofs and tossing his head, affected by his mistress's distress.

'Please stand still, Rufus darling, or we are never going to be away in time.' The saddle safely secure she led the excited horse out of the box. Without waiting for her groom to throw her up she vaulted on to his back. A feat she could not have accomplished if she had not been wearing a divided skirt, an invention of her own. Moments later she was gone, leaving the young man standing, open-mouthed, in the empty stable yard.

Lord Upminster ran into the yard hoping to find his errant bride still there. 'Saddle, Hero,' he ordered. 'No forget that! I will do it myself,' he said to the startled groom. Years of saddling up in seconds meant he was astride and off scarcely minutes after Eleanor had left.

3

The wind whipped Eleanor's hair out from under her hat. Ears flat, neck outstretched, Rufus thundered along, his huge hoofs dislodging clumps of turf. Oblivious to danger, or decorum, she urged the powerful stallion on, their mad gallop suiting the mood of both.

'Steady, boy,' Eleanor called, gently reining in, 'we must meet the next one straight.' The rapidly approaching, dense hedge was at least six foot high and easily four foot wide. It was a formidable obstacle for any but the most experienced and skilled of riders. It presented no problem to Eleanor; the horse responded instantly to the slight check on his reins and gathered himself to jump. She sailed over with inches to spare and continued her ride.

Eventually she became aware of the drum of rapidly approaching hoofbeats. She glanced over her shoulder knowing already who she would see. She crouched and urged Rufus to go faster. There was no horse or rider on this earth, she believed, that could catch her. To her utter astonishment she saw the long grey nose of Hero appear at her heel. Then a hand reached out and caught her rein and her headlong ride was over.

Leo leant back hard in the saddle forcing both horses to slow to a more manageable canter. Eleanor, defeated, also sat back and eased her mount to a standstill. She remained, staring straight ahead, waiting for the storm to break over her head.

'My God, you can ride, Ellie. How much do you want for this horse? He is magnificent.' Leo swung smoothly from the saddle and, looping his reins over his arm, gave Rufus a resounding slap on his heavily sweating neck.

'Nothing, he is not for sale.' Eleanor replied laughing, relieved she was not to have a peal rung over her, and she joined him on the ground. There she flung her arms around her horse's neck and by so doing transferred a large portion of mud to her own face. 'Silly boy. Do not tread on my toes please.' She tried to step back but found that there was a solid obstacle preventing her. Aware, immediately, it was Leo blocking her retreat she froze. She turned to face him.

'Well, little bird, it appears your flight is over.' His voice slid like silk across her muddy face. He placed a fingertip under her chin and tilted her head. 'Look at me, Ellie. Surely you are not afraid?' He smiled down at her, his grey eyes alight with laughter. He drew her into his arms and dropped a gentle kiss on the top of her head.

Involuntarily Eleanor leant back against her horse, away from Leo, startled by his unexpected gesture of affection. Rufus had no wish to act as support to the strangely occupied humans and stepped forward. The solid wall of horseflesh that was supporting their weight, being so abruptly removed, the inevitable happened.

Eleanor started to fall backwards into the space created by the departure of the horse. Leo, still holding her arms was unable to prevent her fall but spun them around and braced himself to take the impact. They landed, with an inelegant thud, on the ground.

'God's teeth!' he swore, as the breath was knocked from his body. 'Bloody animal. Are you all right, Ellie?' he asked, as she struggled to free herself from the tangle of legs and arms they had become. Her flailing limbs were, understandably, making the tangle worse. 'Eleanor, be still.'

Eleanor responded immediately to the authority of his voice and was quiet. Leo sat up taking her with him, and then carefully unravelled the full skirt of her riding habit from around his legs.

'Good girl, now you can stand up.'

Embarrassed, she scrambled to her feet, eager to put as much distance between herself and the smiling giant still spread-eagled on the ground. Leo relieved of his burden sprung lithely to his feet openly laughing at her discomfiture.

'How dare you laugh at me? You ought to be ashamed of yourself. If you had behaved like a gentleman none of this would have happened.'

'Ellie we are engaged to be wed; it is permissible for me to kiss you before our nuptials, you know.'

Eleanor snatched the reins of her mount from his hand and, before he could interfere she had vaulted into the saddle. She glared at her betrothed with dislike. 'That is possibly the case, Lord Upminster, where affections are involved. It is not in a marriage of convenience. I had thought you a man of your word. Perhaps I was mistaken?'

All sign of amusement vanished instantly from Leo's face at this scathing attack on his honour. He stepped up and placed a restraining hand on the bridle of her horse. His eyes held hers and his words were delivered with the same impact as a slap.

'This is the second time today that you have insulted me. There will not be a third

. . . do I make myself clear?'

Her bravado melted under the onslaught of his anger. She gulped nervously, her face devoid of colour. 'Yes, my lord, I apologize.'

'Very well, I will say no more on the subject.' He released his hold and whistled to his own mount, grazing unconcernedly a few yards away. Hero trotted over, ears pricked, eager to return to his stable. Leo sprang into the saddle and, gathering his reins, turned to Eleanor, waiting meekly beside him. 'Come, Eleanor, let us return,' he said, his tone formal. 'We are both in need of a change of clothes and some refreshment.'

The ride back was completed in awkward silence. She had no wish to speak to the formidable man riding beside her; she had experienced two severe set-downs already. Eleanor waited to be dismounted and then hurried off to the house, not wanting to spend a moment longer than she had to in Leo's company.

She had almost reached the rear entrance when she realized the small detail of their wedding had not been discussed. She stopped in her tracks, and then hesitated, unwilling to turn back and initiate a conversation on the subject. She heard a light footfall behind her.

'Stop dithering in the doorway, Eleanor.'

His voice held no trace of his former disapproval.

She decided to risk it. 'My lord, we have to talk.'

'Yes, certainly, but not here, if you please.' He placed his hand in the small of her back and ushered her into the house. She attempted to speak again. 'No, my dear, I refuse to discuss anything in the passageway. Let us repair to the library; we will be private in there.'

A footman materialized at the door and opened it for them. Eleanor was, by now, thoroughly unnerved for Lord Upminster's changes of mood were as random as a weathercock. She marched to the furthest end of the room and sat down on the window seat. He remained standing, eyeing her speculatively from his position in the centre of a handsome Indian rug. He raised an interrogative eyebrow and smiled encouragingly in her direction.

'Why do you wish us to be married today?'

His answer was as brief as her question. 'Until we are wed we are both virtually penniless and there are pressing bills to be paid.'

'But why today? I can not see how a week or two will make much difference.'

He thought for a moment, and then

nodded. 'Very well. I have no wish to cause unhappiness. We will be married in two weeks.'

Eleanor could hardly believe her ears; he had capitulated without demure. Two weeks was not long, indeed she would have preferred longer, but at least it would give her time to assemble a trousseau and find a dress fit for such an important occasion.

'Thank you, my lord. I do understand the urgency of the situation; it is never comfortable to be in debt. But now I will have time to prepare my bride clothes.'

'Bride clothes? Good grief, how could I have been so stupid? I had quite forgotten that young ladies require to refurbish their wardrobes at such a time as this. Please forgive me, Ellie; I promise I will learn to behave more like a civilian and less like a soldier. Just give me time.' His smile of apology made him appear younger and less austere.

There was one more point upon which Eleanor wished to be put straight. 'My lord — ' She got no further as he interrupted her.

'Eleanor, I believe it will be quite acceptable for you to address me by my given name. Even Cousin Leo would do; I am becoming a little tired of your constant, 'my lord's.'

'Very well, my . . . Leo,' she corrected hastily, 'I must suppose that you had already obtained a special licence to allow us to be wed today. As we have now postponed the day are you intending to invite any of your family?'

'It had not occurred to me to do so. But no doubt my brother and his insufferable wife would be delighted to attend. Are you sure you wish me to ask them, they are quite impossible you know?'

Eleanor giggled at his frank appraisal. 'I believe that a wedding with no guests might look a little odd.'

'I do not see why, but I bow to your superior knowledge. No doubt Aunt Prudence brought you up to snuff. She might have been an eccentric, but she was always *au fait* with current fashion, and the ways of the *haut ton*.' He said this with such distaste that Eleanor burst out laughing.

'Did you never go about in town, Leo? Have you never visited Almack's and seen the debutantes on parade?'

Leo's bark of laughter startled her. 'God forbid! I would rather spend an hour having teeth pulled than venture into such a place.' Their conversation was disturbed by a tentative tap on the door. 'Come in,' Leo snapped, displeased by the interruption.

'Excuse me, your lordship,' Brown, the ageing butler, said obsequiously, 'will you be requiring any refreshments to be served?'

'Yes, indeed, thank you. Put out something cold in the yellow drawing-room.' He turned enquiringly to Eleanor. 'Will you be ready to eat in twenty minutes, my dear?'

'Of course, I had not realized how ravenous I was until you mentioned it.'

Brown held open the library door to allow her to pass. As she reached the exit, Leo spoke, his tone still open and friendly.

'Eleanor, it had not escaped my notice that you ride astride, and unaccompanied; you will not do so again. Is that understood?'

She halted; about to make a heated protest, but catching the steely glint in his lordship's grey eyes sensibly refrained from comment.

She took a deep breath and managed a calm, if ambiguous, response. 'I understand perfectly, Leo. Now pray excuse me, or I shall be late.' If she had seen his mouth tighten with annoyance at her pert reply she might not have been so ready to disregard his orders a few days later.

4

'My goodness, miss, whatever's happened? Did you take a tumble?' Eleanor's maid greeted her dishevelled appearance with concern.

'Yes, but not from Rufus, I slipped in the mud when dismounting. It is only my habit that suffered, I assure you.' Eleanor heard Mary muttering under her breath about 'ruining good clothes and skylarking about' as she sank gratefully under the steaming, scented water of her bath.

She lay back, preferring to submerge her shoulders and have her knees above the water, it being impossible to stretch out in the hip-bath prepared for her in the dressing-room. She decided to ask Leo to install one of the new water closets and a bath when they were wed, if he thought to ask what she wanted for a bride gift.

Reluctantly she stepped out and allowed Mary to envelop her in a warm bath sheet. 'Lord Upminster and I are to be married two weeks today. Will we be able to make up sufficient new gowns and undergarments by then?'

'Lawks, Miss Ellie! I know you are a marvel with the shears and needle but a whole trousseau in two weeks? We will never do it on our own!'

Eleanor laughed as she dried herself briskly. 'I know that. I thought I would employ some women from the village and also get the help of any housemaids who can sew.' She quickly donned her clean white undergarments, glad the new fashion no longer necessitated that a girl as slim as she was had to wear a restricting corset. The high-waisted, loosely flowing lines of the current fashion admirably suited her tall, slender build. The pale-green sprigged muslin worn over an underskirt of yellow silk was a fine example of a gown she had cut and made herself.

The pictures displayed in such publications as *La Belle Assemblée* had always been sufficient inspiration for her to cut and make what she needed, and to remain in the forefront of the present mode. Lovely in a gown that matched the green of her eyes Eleanor hurried out of the room, unwilling to miss a meal for the second time in as many hours.

The food had been set out on small tables, as instructed, in the yellow drawing-room. It was the room both Lady Dunston and

Eleanor preferred to use when they had no guests. In spite of her rush, Leo was there before her.

'At last; I don't think I could have lasted another minute without sustenance.' The rebuke was spoken teasingly and she could not take offence.

'I must apologize, my . . . Leo, it is always so hard to leave the comfort of one's bath.' She stopped, appalled, her face crimson. How could she have been so immodest as to mention her bath? Nobly Leo kept his face straight and refrained from commenting.

'I have been thinking about your trousseau. Even I know enough to realize that fashionable gowns and fripperies do not come cheap.'

Eleanor interrupted him, glad that for once she could have something to say that would please him. 'Do you mean a gown like this, Leo?' She spun round allowing the daffodil yellow under-slip to show beneath the green.

'Indeed I do. It's a beautiful confection, Ellie, and must have cost your Aunt Prudence a small fortune.'

Eleanor crowed with delight. 'You are wrong! This dress cost almost nothing, I made it myself.'

If Eleanor had announced she was a devil worshipper Leo could not have been more astonished. 'I do not understand. My . . . ' Leo hesitated, considering it indelicate to mention the name of his most recent ladybird in front of his betrothed. 'My brother has often repined that the cost of keeping his wife at the pinnacle of fashion is bankrupting him. Why does Sophia not make her own clothes and save them a fortune?'

Eleanor shook her head, his ignorance of matters female not surprising her in the least. 'I am an exception, Leo; there are few women of rank who would have the skill, or the wish, to do as I have done.' Relaxed in his company for the first time she led the way over to the enticing spread. 'Shall we eat as we talk? It looks delicious and I for one could eat a bear.'

Leo chuckled at her unladylike expression. 'Minx,' he said affectionately, 'be seated and I will bring you a plate.'

Finally replete, Eleanor dropped her cutlery noisily. 'I could not eat another morsel. I do hope Brown has the sense to delay dinner; it is almost three now and I am certain I will be unable to contemplate further food a moment earlier than eight o'clock.'

Leo finished his last forkful of game pie before replying. 'I admit that Brown is somewhat stiff and formal but he is neither unobservant, nor a fool. I am sure that when he sees what inroads we have made, he will draw his own conclusions and ask Cook to make the necessary adjustments in the kitchen.' He pushed his empty plate away, stood up and offered his hand to Eleanor. 'Come, Ellie, shall we sit by the fire? You can reveal to me the secrets of a top modiste.' Eleanor declined to take his outstretched hand; she didn't like the strange sensation such contact aroused.

'There are no secrets my . . . Leo.' She was finding it hard to use his given name. 'I discovered in India that I had a talent for design and dressmaking. Material is inexpensive and plentiful out there and Aunt Prudence and I spent weeks wandering in and out of bazaars buying silks, cottons, muslins and all the threads, braid and ribbons to complement them.' She glanced across to check that her long speech, on so feminine a subject, had not sent his lordship to sleep with boredom.

He smiled encouragement. 'Go on, I am absolutely riveted.'

'Humbug!' she exclaimed giggling. 'But you did ask so I will complete my tale. There was little to do during the hot afternoons except sleep. So I learnt to cut and sew and then, as I became expert, to make all our new clothes. Mary, and Smith, Aunt Prudence's abigail, did the bulk of the sewing. My task was mainly to design, cut and finish.'

'I am impressed,' he said, and he meant it. 'I imagine there can be few ladies of quality who have such a talent. You made your own wardrobe from choice, rather than necessity?'

'Of course, but as you know I grew up in different circumstances to these. I learned to economize and make do very early in life. Although Papa's income was modest we managed quite well. I could never be comfortable living in excessive luxury when others under my protection did without.'

'Noble sentiments, my dear, but you had best keep your radical thoughts to yourself in company.'

Eleanor looked, with exaggerated care, around the empty room. 'I was not aware that we had company, but I assure you that when we do, I will refrain from commenting on the lamentable conditions in which many of the tenants of wealthy landowners are forced to live.' This was a matter dear to her heart and not even Upminster's disapproval would stop her expressing her feelings.

Leo raised his hands in a gesture of surrender. 'Enough, little firebrand. I am on your side; you are preaching to the converted.'

'You are?' Eleanor's face was illuminated

by her smile. 'I had not realized. I am so glad you agree with me. There is so much good we can do once Aunt Prudence's legacy is released.'

'This returns us nicely to an original point. I have spoken to the vicar, and a letter is on its way to invite my brother and his wife to attend the ceremony. Will you be ready in two weeks?'

'The matter is already in hand.' She smiled, a second time, in his direction quite unaware of the effect she was having on him. 'Or at least it will be if you will excuse me to attend to it.' She rose gracefully as she spoke.

Leo surged to his feet and bowed politely. 'I will see you at dinner, Eleanor. I have business to see to, but will be in the study if you need me.'

★   ★   ★

Ten minutes later, Eleanor and her maid crept quietly up the back stairs, each carrying a candelabrum, not wishing to attract the attention of the servants. Eleanor wished to search through the trunks of exotic garments and materials that were stored in the attic.

Brown would be scandalized by her intention. No lady of quality would dream of visiting such a place; a footman would be sent to remove the trunks for her. That course would take too long and she was determined to find the things she needed immediately. The attic door opened easily with no squeaking to alert a watchful servant.

'Give me your candles, Mary. I will hold them up so you can see.' The combined light flooded the space, allowing them to explore to the furthest corner. The steeply pitched roof meant that only the centre of the room was tall enough for Eleanor to stand upright. Mary, a head shorter, was able to search more easily, the danger of banging her head much less.

'Here we are. I have found the ones we want, Miss Ellie. There must be a dozen stacked away over here.'

Eleanor carefully balanced the candelabrum on a nearby shelf and joined Mary on the floor. The trunk lids were flung back eagerly, the resulting clatter ignored in her eagerness to examine the contents.

'What in God's name are you doing up here?' Leo had been dragged from his work by the information that there were burglars in the attic. And as Sam, his manservant, had already been sent on an errand, he had to investigate the matter himself.

Startled, Eleanor jumped up and cracked her head on a beam. 'Ouch! That hurt

. . . that really hurt,' she moaned, and sank back to the floor, clutching her head dramatically in her hands.

Leo was immediately contrite. 'Here, Ellie, let me see. What have you done?' He tried, gently, to prise her hands away. 'Please, little one, I cannot help you, if you will not let me look.' He spoke soothingly, as though to a small child injured in a playtime fall.

Eleanor looked up, removing her hands as she did so. She glared directly into Leo's sympathetic eyes. 'Go away, Leo, there's nothing wrong with my head. I was merely demonstrating to you the stupidity of yelling and scaring a person half to death.'

He sat back on his heels, unable to decide whether he was exasperated or amused by her antics. He smiled. 'Ellie, you are an idiot! You could have hurt yourself.'

'Exactly! So please keep the parade-ground voice for your soldiers, in future, my lord,' she replied, her smile quite disarming him.

Leo sighed. 'I give in. I am sorry I shouted at you. Next time I find you rummaging through old clothes in the attic, giving an excellent impression of a burglar, I will enquire politely, and quietly, what on earth you are doing.'

'Burglar? Did you think we were burglars? How ridiculous! As if a burglar could get up here, in daytime, without being seen! I've never . . . ' She collapsed, unable to continue, made helpless by laughter.

He scowled at the giggling girl, sitting cross-legged in front of him, totally unfazed by his frown. He got to his feet, deftly avoiding the beams, and stood staring down at Eleanor, a puzzled expression on his face.

He shrugged. 'I will leave you to your work,' he said a little stiffly. 'Is there anything I can do for you before I depart?'

'Thank you; could you arrange for some footmen to carry these trunks down to the ballroom.'

'Ballroom?' He shrugged, puzzled by the request.

Eleanor attempted to rise, finding she was acquiring a crick in the neck conversing with Leo from her position on the floor. Unfortunately her dress had become entangled around her feet and she pitched, headfirst into him. For the second time that day they fell full length on the floor, Eleanor's soft feminine curves trapped against his hard athletic body.

'Good God, Ellie! You are beginning to make a habit of this!' Leo exclaimed, when he had recovered his breath. Eleanor opened her eyes to find them inches away from his. The feel of his arms holding her steady, and the touch of his warm breath on her cheeks was sending her blood fizzing around her body.

They both heard a small, discreet cough from above them. 'Excuse me, Miss Eleanor, are you hurt by your fall?' Mary enquired, aware that her young mistress was in a very compromising position.

Leo gently pushed Ellie aside, then regained his feet and pulled her up beside him, fully aware of the effect he had had on his betrothed. 'I am sorry, my dear,' he said, stepping firmly away. 'If you are unhurt, I will go at once and organize the men to remove the trunks.'

5

Inclement weather for the next few days meant that Eleanor was able to devote all her time to the construction of her bride clothes. The ballroom now resembled a dressmaker's workshop. She had even discovered that the wife of the village blacksmith had been a milliner for a prestigious London emporium and the woman was more than happy to make as many poke or chip-straw bonnets as required.

Already her willing band of seamstresses had made all the petticoats, camisoles, pantelettes and nightrails that she would require. Also finished were a second riding habit, three walking dresses with matching pelisses and three day dresses in Indian muslin. Almost complete was her first fashionable evening gown. The girls were hurrying to stitch the cream silk gown that Eleanor was intending to wear for her wedding.

'I do believe it has stopped raining at last, I am desperate for some fresh air and exercise after being cooped up in here for days.'

Mary immediately left her sewing to join

her mistress at the French doors. 'It will still be wet underfoot, miss; you will ruin your boots.'

'I am not going to walk, I am going to ride. Rufus must be as eager as I am to get out into the sunshine.'

★ ★ ★

Less than twenty minutes later, Eleanor arrived in the stable yard. She had not forgotten that she was forbidden to ride her horse astride and ordered the groom to fetch a suitable side saddle.

'He don't like the looks of this, Miss Eleanor,' John warned, watching the huge chestnut horse back away, stamping his hoofs angrily.

'Let me do it. Maybe he will be quieter for me.' She approached her horse, speaking softly to him as she advanced. 'There . . . there . . . Rufus; steady boy, I have nothing here that will hurt you.'

The horse settled at the soothing sound of her voice and he allowed her to place the side saddle on his back. The girth was quickly fastened and the single leather adjusted to fit.

'Up you go, Miss Eleanor,' John said, and expertly tossed her into the saddle. Eleanor had no time to place her foot in the iron or shorten her reins, before Rufus exploded. The unaccustomed shape, and strange stance of his rider, was too much for his fiery nature. Bucking and cavorting he shot across the yard depositing Eleanor on the cobbles as he did so. From her undignified position on the ground, she pulled hard at the reins and spoke sharply to the frightened horse.

'Be quiet, Rufus. Enough, stand boy . . . stand.' The stallion froze in mid buck, suddenly aware that his beloved owner was speaking to him from beneath his hoofs. His head came up from between his legs and he nuzzled Eleanor, puzzled by her unexpected position.

'Stupid horse,' she scolded crossly, and pushed his nose away. The terrified groom appeared by her side and, unsure whether to take the horse or assist her to her feet, attempted to do both and succeeded in neither. Rufus, freshly startled, snatched the reins from his hand.

Eleanor scrambled to her feet ignoring John's tentative gesture. Once again she spoke steadily to the horse. 'Stand still, Rufus. Stand.' The horse calmed and waited quietly for her to gather his reins firmly in one hand. She patted his sweaty neck and made soothing noises. The hated side saddle was now hanging askew. 'Remove this and put my normal one on please, John. I do not think it will be possible to ride side saddle after all.'

'Yes, Miss Eleanor, right away,' he replied, relieved she was not going to risk another fall. Rufus was re-saddled in minutes and John, for the second time, tossed Eleanor aboard. He mounted on a showy bay hack and they set off together; he following a respectful distance behind.

Eleanor knew she had ignored Leo's instructions but felt she had had no option. If her horse would not accept a side saddle then there was little she could do; no one else could ride him safely and the horse needed to be exercised. As she was not riding unaccompanied she had only disobeyed one instruction, after all.

* * *

She had a glorious ride, the going perfect for galloping and jumping. When she returned to the stable two hours later the watery, late October, sun was setting. Leaving John to take care of Rufus she ran back along the path praying fervently that her escapade had gone unnoticed.

The long corridor was empty; no sign of an enraged fiancé waiting to reprimand her for her actions. 'Thank goodness,' she whispered, 'I am undetected. It is possible that now I will be able to explain what happened. Maybe he will understand why I had to disobey him.'

She slipped quietly up the back stairs and hurried into her bedchamber. Mary had left her bath, gently steaming, in front of the dressing-room fire, and her clean garments were ready on the stand. Without waiting for her abigail to answer the summons of the bell, Eleanor undressed and stepped into her waiting water.

Mary arrived a few minutes later, her face pale. 'Oh miss, why did you do it? His lordship is so angry with you.'

Eleanor's heart sank and she shivered in spite of the warm water and roaring fire. 'How can he know? Who could have told him?' She got out as she spoke and grabbed the towel from Mary's outstretched hand.

'Not half an hour ago he came to the ballroom to speak to you and when he discovered you had gone riding he went off to find you. He must have seen you. No one would carry tales to him, you know that.'

'I do not see how he could have done, not without me knowing.' Then she remembered. 'He would have seen that the man's saddle had gone and the side saddle was still there.' She frowned, and then smiled ruefully. 'It is too late for speculation. I must go down and face the music. I do hope he has calmed down a little.'

Mary refrained from reminding her that he had only just discovered Eleanor's disobedience and his rage would have had no time to abate.

To a casual observer, Eleanor presented the appearance of fashionable young lady without a care in the world. Her face reflected none of the panic she felt at the thought of her forthcoming interview with the irascible colonel. Her legs were trembling as she walked sedately to the library and she feared her hands would be shaking too much to allow her to open the door. She knocked, wishing that she could disappear, be anywhere but there.

'Come in,' Leo commanded. She pushed open the solid wooden door and stepped in, her head held high, determined not to show how frightened she was.

'I gather you wish to see me, Leo,' she said politely, stepping into the library.

Leo strode down the room towards her, his face set, his eyes as cold as the sea.

'Do not stand there, Eleanor. Come in and close the door. What I have to say to you, I wish to say in private.'

She walked across the room and sat down

on a straight backed hard chair, thankful her shaking legs had managed to carry her that far. He followed her, but did not sit; instead he turned and faced her, his back to the gently crackling fire.

He opened his attack without preamble. 'I expressly told you not to ride astride; you disobeyed me.' His expression was grim and Eleanor decided now was not the time to offer an explanation. She hung her head, hoping her apologetic posture would soften his heart. It did not. 'It is too late for remorse, young lady. As your legal guardian, and your fiancé, I have a right to be obeyed. Look at me.'

Miserably she raised her head and met his eyes. She flinched from the anger there. 'I have decided that you will not ride at all until I give you leave. Not astride, not side saddle, not at all. Do I make myself clear?'

'Not ride? You cannot mean that!'

'I mean it. All the grooms have been told that if they have the temerity to disobey, they will be turned off, instantly.'

Eleanor was aghast. She was the only one who could ride her stallion; he trusted and loved her. How would he feel if she abandoned him, to stand in his loose box all day and every day? He had been used for stud during her long absence and it had taken weeks to accustom him to being ridden again. Her face reflected her worry and Leo watched, his mouth tight, his expression uncompromising.

'And,' he continued harshly, 'I would strongly advise you to forget any plan you might have to tack-up for yourself.' His eyes bored into hers and she was unable to look away. 'I have never raised my hand to a female but will not hesitate to do so if I am disobeyed again, Eleanor.'

'You would beat me? Are you saying you would beat me if I do not do as you say?' Her voice was scarcely above a whisper.

'That is exactly what I am saying. If you persist in behaving like a spoilt brat you can expect to be treated as one.' He turned his back on her thus ending the conversation.

Eleanor, chastened beyond belief, slipped out of the room, her tears spilling unchecked down her ashen cheeks. Knowing that Mary would be waiting in her bedchamber, she fled along the corridor and out through the side door into the garden, desperate to find a place of solitude; to hide away to cry out her misery in private.

She ran across the grass, her silk slippers soaked in seconds and the hem of her dress dragging in the damp. Exhausted, she collapsed inside a hidden arbour at the far end of the extensive rose garden and dropped her head into her hands. She was not crying because she was unable to ride, that was a hardship she could endure; she was not crying because her beloved horse would go unexercised, she knew a groom could turn him out. No, she was weeping for her lost dream.

Her marriage was never going to become a union based on love and respect. How could she ever live happily with a man who would impose his will by physical force? She knew that a husband had the right, in law, to chastize his wife, but never dreamt that Leo would wish to exercise that right. Then she remembered the unkind words she had overheard, three years before, and her sorrow turned to anger.

The tears dried on her face. 'How dare he talk to me like that? I am not his daughter and neither am I his wife, yet. I am nineteen years of age and I will not be bullied by a redundant soldier.' She had spoken aloud, and her words gave her courage. She stood up, suddenly aware that she was shivering, not from fear as before, but from cold. The sun had fully set and a soft persistent rain had started to fall.

Eleanor left the safety of her hiding place and hurried back through the rapidly darkening garden, well aware that her prolonged stay outside, in nothing more than a thin muslin dress, was hardly sensible. She ran the risk of sustaining a head cold, or even worse, if she didn't get into warm, dry clothes soon.

She hoped to be able to slip back indoors and gain the security of her bedchamber without further confrontation. As she stepped, a bedraggled and miserable picture, through the side entrance she came face to face with the one person she most wished to avoid.

'Sweet heaven! Where have you been, Ellie?' Leo's voice was full of concern, his face etched with worry. 'Look at you; you are soaked and shaking with cold.' Not waiting for an answer he swept her up into his arms and carried her, too tired and cold to protest, upstairs, where Mary waited with warm clothes and a hot drink. He shouldered his way in and placed Eleanor gently down in front of the roaring fire. 'Little idiot,' he growled. 'Why did you run off like that?'

She lifted her white face and said bitterly, 'You said you would beat me. How can I marry someone who would do that to me?'

Leo pulled her into his arms roughly and hugged her fiercely. 'I was angry. I have the devil's own temper and I spoke out of turn; I

49

am not used to being gainsaid. I would not hurt you, little bird, whatever I might say. I will never raise a hand to you, I give you my word.'

Eleanor wriggled out of his embrace. 'But I believed you, Leo. You frightened me.'

'I am sorry, Ellie. I should not have threatened you, it was wrong.' He gave her a little shake. 'But, my dear, my instruction still stands, you will not ride until I give you leave.' She opened her mouth to protest, but seeing his expression, decided to remain silent. 'I will leave you to change; I will see you at dinner, we need to talk.'

Eleanor allowed Mary to strip the sodden garments from her, but her mind was far away, trying to adjust to yet another change in her relationship. One minute he was threatening to beat her, the next, holding her close to his heart and calling her, 'my dear'. What was going on? He would have to decide whether he wished to treat her as a woman grown or a child. She would not allow him to continue to confuse her like this.

6

Dinner was to be served at the fashionable hour of eight o'clock, much to the dismay of the staff, all more used to country ways. Eleanor had spent an hour or so resting in her bed with a hot brick at her feet, not wishing to catch a chill from her soaking. Mary woke her with a cup of hot chocolate.

'What time is it, Mary? I must have fallen asleep.'

'It's almost seven, miss, plenty of time before the dinner gong. Have you decided what you wish to wear tonight?'

'It is a shame my new rose crepe dinner gown is not completed; I would have liked to wear that.'

'But it is, Miss Ellie. One of the girls finished the hem this afternoon and I pressed it whilst you were resting.'

Eleanor jumped out of bed, her drink disregarded on the side table. 'Let me see it please.'

Mary held it up for inspection. The dark-rose silk crepe had been designed to fit tight over her bosom and the tiny cap sleeves were exquisitely embroidered with dainty

51

rosettes made from ruby red bugle-beads. The décolleté was quite daring and decorated in the same style as the sleeves. The skirt fell in shimmering folds, the beads embroidered on it swirling from bodice to hem and the back was finished with a small train.

'How beautiful, Mary. I cannot believe it has turned out as well as this. Are you sure the red beads are not too much? After all, red is considered rather a fast colour.' It was a sophisticated dress, a dinner dress for an adult and Eleanor was unsure whether she was ready to wear it.

'It is perfect, lovey, and it will look perfect on you. My, you'll have his lordship's eyes out on stalks when you go down in this.'

Eleanor was not quite sure she wanted Leo to have such a reaction. When he looked at her in that sort of way she became flustered and hot. She thought she preferred him angry, then at least, she knew where she was.

The gown, as expected, looked even better on. Mary put Eleanor's hair up in a knot on top of her head, allowing a few curls to escape each side. They had found a necklace of deep ruby-red garnets, and matching ear-drops, which complemented the outfit admirably. The ensemble was completed with elbow-length gloves in the exact shade of the beads, and rose crepe slippers embroidered to match.

She stood, enchanted, in front of the full-length glass. Eleanor knew the dress made her appear beautiful; she felt like an exotic foreign princess, not like herself at all. The dinner gong sounded, the harsh noise reverberating throughout the house. For once Eleanor was eager to go down; she couldn't wait to see Leo's reaction to her new finery.

She glided down the stairs, her feet barely touching the steps, her head high and her eyes sparkling. Leo was waiting in the hall, his back to her, staring pensively into the fire.

'I am sorry if I have kept you waiting, Leo.' Eleanor spoke softly as she came towards him. He turned slowly to face her and stopped, arrested, his eyes widened and his jaw dropped.

'My God, you look ravishing, my dear.' He took her hand in his and raised it to his lips. The gentle touch of his mouth sent a flash of heat down her arm. She had hoped to make an impression, to show she was no longer a child, but she was finding the darkness in Leo's eyes was equally disturbing.

Eleanor removed her hand. 'This is the first of my new dinner gowns. I am glad it meets with your approval.' Her voice was light, accepting his compliment as a well-bred young lady should. 'I adore this dress, Leo; look how lovely the skirt is when I move.' She twirled around like a child making her dress spin out in a pink cloud around her.

Leo laughed, the darkness went and his eyes were a clear, slate-grey again. 'It is a truly wonderful gown and if you could only behave for longer than five minutes, one could almost mistake you for a grown-up.'

Ellie's delighted gurgle of laughter accompanied them into the dining-room. The dinner was, as usual, elaborate and delicious, with several removes and side dishes. Late though it was, both Eleanor and Leo found they had sufficient appetite to do it justice. They had been chattering companionably across the table on various innocuous subjects when Ellie decided it was safe to mention the events of the afternoon.

'Leo, I wish to explain to you what happened this afternoon,' she began, hoping he would allow her to continue.

He frowned at her. 'I think it is a subject that is best left alone, my dear.'

'Please, I would like to tell you why I disobeyed you.'

Her earnest expression convinced him she had something other than excuses to offer. 'Very well, Eleanor, if you insist, but I give you fair warning that you are more likely to earn my approbation than my understanding.'

She smiled nervously but decided to risk his disapproval anyway. Leo listened impassively until she told him of her fall. His eyes flashed dangerously and his face darkened.

'You could have been injured. That damned horse is too much for you. You should not be riding it.'

'No, he is not. He has never thrown me before. It was the saddle; I should have realized he would not like it.'

'Am I to understand that this was the first time that animal had met a side saddle?'

'Of course it was. Why should he have had on a side saddle, as I am the only person who rides him?'

Leo shook his head in disbelief, not sure whether to laugh or get up and shake some sense into the idiotic girl sitting opposite. 'Good God! How could such an experienced horsewoman fail to realize that the introduction of any new tack requires skill and patience? No horse, however docile, would accept a new saddle without preparation.'

Eleanor stared at Leo, her eyes wide with shock. 'Rufus has always done as I ask. I am afraid it never occurred to me he would object, or I would have done things differently. It is no wonder he was upset.'

'You,' he said, smiling broadly, 'as I have said before, are a complete ninny, Eleanor, my child. I blame myself for not realizing it sooner.'

At her look of indignation his smile became a deep roar of laughter. He leant forward in his chair shaking with amusement. His behaviour incensed Eleanor still further.

'It was your stupid idea to ride him with a side saddle, pray do not forget that! If I had not been carrying out your instructions I would not have fallen, would I?' Her voice had risen and she was almost shouting.

Leo mopped his streaming eyes and reached across to capture her wildly waving hands. 'Please, my dear, do not raise your voice; it is so very unbecoming.'

She snatched her hands away and replied haughtily, 'I believe that if I mention a pot and a kettle, my lord, you will fully take my meaning.'

He bowed, and the charm of the smile he bestowed upon her was quite devastating. '*Touché*, my angel; I stand corrected.'

'But you do not,' she teased, by now thoroughly enjoying their repartee.

'Do not what?'

'Do not *stand corrected* . . . as you are sitting you can hardly *stand corrected*, can you?'

'And you, my girl, will find yourself unable to sit at all if you persist in this nonsense.' His eyes were alight with laughter as he spoke.

'You gave your word you would not raise your hand to me, so fiddlesticks to that,' she answered rather rashly.

'A hand, yes, but I do not believe anything was said about the use of a hairbrush was it?' His expression was serious and, for an awful moment, Eleanor believed him. She pushed back her chair and, leaping to her feet, prepared to flee the room, in case he truly desired to carry out his threat.

'Sit down, Ellie, it was a joke. However much you might deserve a spanking I will endeavour to restrain myself from administering it.'

'So I should hope. I am not a child, Leo, and do not take kindly to being treated as one.'

'Just how would you like to be treated?' he asked, his eyes narrowing speculatively. This time Eleanor recognized the danger signals.

'With the same respect that I treat you, Leo. If this marriage of convenience is to work we must show mutual respect.'

'Calling me, now let me think *an idiot* and *a pot* are considered respectful, are they?'

'No, but calling me *a ninny* and *a baggage*, are hardly the height of politeness.'

'Shall we call it quits then? And both promise to improve our manners?'

Eleanor's smile was captivating. 'I believe I could almost be starting to like you, Leo, in spite of your many faults.'

'Are you indeed? How very kind of you to say so, and I, of course, find you quite irresistible, my love, especially when you are showing me so much respect.'

'I am going to leave you to your port. I have bandied quite enough nonsense with you this evening, Leo.' She stood up and began to walk towards the door when he called her back.

'I will join you in the drawing-room later, Ellie.'

She smiled saucily over her shoulder at the dark, attractive man, standing, watching her. 'That is your prerogative, I believe, my lord.' Before he could answer she skipped out, scarcely allowing the footman time to open the door.

★   ★   ★

Eleanor decided to escape to the library instead of waiting for Leo to join her for tea in the drawing-room. She found a book that she hadn't read and curled up contentedly in an armchair in front of the fire. She had only read a few pages when the excitement and emotional strain of the day overcame her, and her eyes closed slowly and her book dropped to the floor, unnoticed.

It was there that Leo found her, fast asleep, some twenty minutes later. Smiling down at the sweetly sleeping girl, he was loath to wake her. She looked so adorable that all the irritation he had felt at her defection, quite evaporated. He scooped her out of the chair easily and carried her from the library and up to her bedchamber.

7

When Eleanor awoke the next morning, still in her undergarments, she was puzzled. Then she remembered that she had fallen asleep in the library, so how had she ended up in bed? Leo must have carried her up; she glanced down at her *déshabillé* in shock. Surely he hadn't been the one to remove her evening dress?

She reached over and pulled the bell cord, hard. Only Mary could explain what had happened and Ellie needed to know the truth as soon as possible. She heard her maid coming in through the dressing-room door, followed by the chambermaid, carrying the jug of hot water for her morning ablutions.

Mary entered with the usual tray of hot chocolate and soft, sweet rolls. 'Good morning, Miss Ellie. Did you sleep well?' She stopped, shocked by what she saw. 'Good heavens, you are still in your petticoats! Why ever didn't you call me? I know it was my evening off but I was only in with Mrs Beaconsfield having a game of whist.'

Eleanor felt her face glowing pink with embarrassment. If Mary hadn't undressed her then Leo must have. How absolutely dreadful! How mortifying; she was never going to be able to face him with equanimity again. She realized Mary was waiting expectantly for her answer.

'I did not like to disturb you. It cannot hurt to sleep in one's undergarments occasionally, can it? I was too fatigued to struggle with all the buttons and ribbons on my own.'

'It is a good thing Lady Dunston is not here to know about it, is all I can say,' Mary said, obviously still bothered by Eleanor's shocking lack of decorum.

'I will wear one of my new gowns today. I think that the peach and brown sarcenet, with the organdie overskirt, would be perfect for an autumn day.' Mary's reply was grumpy, and Eleanor realized it would take considerably longer for her abigail to forgive her lapse.

She was glad to remove herself from the confines of her bedchamber. Her maid's sunny disposition had temporarily disappeared because of the degrading spectacle her charge had presented, asleep in her underwear like a demi-rep. Eleanor giggled as she closed the door behind her. Whatever was becoming of her ladylike pretensions? In less than two weeks she had descended into shouting matches over the table, rummaging in boxes in the attic, and, to cap it all, sleeping in her underwear!

Lord Upminster was quite definitely a bad influence and his language was quite shocking. She knew she had always been what was politely known as, a lively girl, but now she feared she was rapidly deteriorating into what could only be described as, a sad romp. She paused at the top of the stairs. The shining, gently curving banister gleamed invitingly.

Eleanor had not slid down it since she was fourteen and newly arrived to live at Monk's Hall. Dare she do it one more time before she became a staid, married lady? Yes, she could. Without further hesitation she swung her leg over the rail and launched herself.

She had forgotten just how fast one travelled on a slippery polished surface and, almost immediately, deeply regretted her impulse. By the time she arrived at the halfway point she was feeling decidedly unstable and knew, with a sickening certainty that this particular escapade was going to end in disaster. As she felt herself swaying dangerously she cried out, instinctively calling for Leo.

'Leo, Leo . . . help me please, I am falling!' she screamed as she hurtled towards the hard parquet floor of the entrance hall. At the very last possible moment two strong arms encircled her waist and she was snatched from the banister.

Leo staggered backwards, trying desperately to keep his balance. The speed of her descent was almost too much for him. With a painful thud he crashed against the wall, his fall halted by the impact. Carefully he restored Eleanor to her feet.

'What the devil were you thinking of, you stupid girl? You could have been killed.' He grabbed her shoulders and was preparing to give her the shaking she richly deserved when he heard a small, ominous, gulping noise. He looked down at Eleanor's sickly green face with alarm. 'Outside! Hold on, sweetheart.' He snatched her up and ran for the door, hastily opened by Brown. He made it in the nick of time.

'Oh please put me down, Leo. I am going to be horribly sick.' And so saying, she was. Leo held her hair away from her face and offered her his support until the awful retching had ceased. When it was over he wiped her mouth with his pristine white handkerchief and held her gently against him.

'How do you feel now?'

'Better, thank you. I am so sorry . . . '

'Forget it. Just promise me, never, ever do anything so stupid again.'

Eleanor drew a deep, steadying breath. 'I

promise. I have never been so scared in my life; Leo, I thought I was going to be killed. Whatever possessed me to do such a thing?'

'God knows; I said you were a ninny and after this morning's performance, my dear, I hold by that assessment.'

'I think I would like to go for a walk, my head is still spinning a little.'

He pulled her arm through his and smiled down at her affectionately. 'Well, I suppose a walk is fairly harmless, but I still think I had better accompany you in case you have any other harebrained schemes in mind.' He kept on talking in a friendly, light-hearted manner, hoping his words would take away the fear he could still see in her eyes.

They strolled around the rose garden admiring the few blooms that remained, but Eleanor's responses remained subdued. Leo halted by the arched entrance to the stable yard, worried by the continuing silence.

'Ellie, what is it, sweetheart? Are you feeling unwell?' She mumbled an incoherent reply and attempted to withdraw her arm from his. Leo held her by the shoulders and studied her pale face closely. 'Cut rope, Eleanor. There is something troubling you — tell me what it is. For we will not move from here until you do so.' Although his tone was kindly there was no doubt he meant every word.

'Last night . . . ' She felt herself blushing again as she spoke. 'Last night . . . Leo, you should not have done it,' she finally managed to say. The look of astonishment that flashed across his face was closely followed by a thunderous expression.

He dropped his hands from her shoulders as if he had been burnt by the contact. 'I hope you are not suggesting that I behaved in anyway improperly, Eleanor?'

'No, that is . . . ' she stumbled, confused by his reaction. This will not do, she castigated herself, I am the victim here, not the culprit. 'I am suggesting, my lord, that you undressed me last night. That action was totally unacceptable.'

'Good God, Ellie, is that all?' He grinned, the grim expression vanishing. 'I thought you were accusing me of ravishing you in your sleep.'

Eleanor didn't know whether to laugh, or be outraged, at his frank speaking. 'You should have rung for my abigail; you have placed me in an embarrassing situation.'

'Come on, Ellie, you are making too much fuss over a trifle. I saw you in your undergarments, not unclothed. It would be quite a different matter if I was not to be your husband in less than a week.'

Eleanor felt the conversation was taking a direction she didn't care for. 'Not a true husband, remember; it is a marriage of convenience only and, as such, I must insist that there are no further intimacies of that kind.' Her speech sounded, even to her ears, pompous and silly.

He ruffled her hair. 'Do not fret, little bird, you can fly free for a while longer.' And with that cryptic statement he clasped her arm to his and led the way under the arch to the stable yard.

The sound of impatiently stamping hoofs echoed round the empty yard. Eleanor let go of Leo's arm and rushed over to the loose box in which her precious horse was housed.

'Rufus, whatever is the matter? Stop that noise right now,' she admonished him sternly. Immediately the stamping ceased and a handsome chestnut head emerged over the loose-box door. Eleanor rubbed his muzzle lovingly and the horse lipped her arm, delighted to see his mistress.

Leo joined her and pulled the horse's ears. 'I expect you are bored, old fellow; missing your gallops, are you?' He looked thoughtfully from Eleanor, to the stallion standing so peacefully beside her and came to a decision. 'Very well, I relent. You can ride this monster again, but only with me, and never when we have company.'

Eleanor was overjoyed; without thinking she spun round and flung her arms about him, intending only to reward him with a friendly hug. However, offered such an un-expected opportunity, he enclosed her slim frame with arms of steel. He drew her closer, welding their bodies together. Eleanor could not step back, even if she had wished to do so.

She tilted her head instinctively, knowing full well what the result would be. Leo's mouth claimed hers in a searing kiss; his lips moved almost roughly against hers, then one hand came up to cup her head, forcing it back to allow him to plunder her mouth still further. She parted her lips in order to catch her breath but Leo took this chance to deepen the kiss to a level that swept her away from all safe places to experience a flood of uncharted feelings.

'Alas, my love, I think this has gone quite far enough,' he said presently, releasing her, and gazing down ruefully into her dazed face. 'If you do not wish to be kissed, my dear Ellie, please refrain from flinging yourself so precipitously into my arms.'

Eleanor finally found her voice. 'That is the outside of enough, Leo. How dare you suggest that I was encouraging you to kiss me? My embrace was as a friend, and you took shameful advantage of me.'

He smiled, unrepentant. 'Quite possibly, but then I am a man, and full of the baser instincts.' He strode off in the direction of the house causing Eleanor to run to catch up with him.

'That is no excuse, Leo,' she told him firmly. 'You must learn to control your impulses, as I do.'

Leo's shout of laughter startled the sparrows from their roost in the tall bay hedge beside the path. Still chuckling, he said, as they entered the house, 'I will promise to control my impulses if you promise to control yours.'

This sounded vaguely familiar to Ellie. Hadn't they made a similar promise the previous night? Why did he go out of his way to confuse her? 'I believe we have already promised to improve our manners, now we are to promise to control our impulses. I do declare, Lord Upminster, that we shall hardly know ourselves if we continue to improve our characters in this way,' she replied archly, determined not to let him have the last word again.

Leo halted allowing her to cannon into his solid back. He reached round and taking her hands lifted them to his lips to imprint his mouth upon her tingling palms. 'You are playing a dangerous game here, Ellie, my love; you are in over your head. If you are sincere in wishing our relationship to remain platonic it would be wiser if you stopped flirting with me. You are a lovely young woman and I am not made of stone.' He released her hands and left her standing, bemused by his actions, and half afraid, half excited by his words.

She realized that they had not agreed on a time for their ride and Leo's lengthy strides were carrying him rapidly out of sight. Forgetting all her promises to behave like a young lady, she yelled after him. 'Leo, please wait a moment.'

He paused, his long fingers clutching the banisters as if they were a lifeline. 'Yes, Eleanor, what is it now?' His tone reflected his vexation. She arrived in a rush at his side.

'Are we to ride immediately?'

'Yes, I was, as you can see, on my way upstairs to change.'

'Excellent, shall I meet you here in ten minutes?'

'Yes, Eleanor. And please refrain from screeching down the corridor like a fish wife,' he told her, with little hope that she would heed his words.

'I am sorry, but you were so far away you would not have heard otherwise.'

'Eleanor, you are incorrigible! To think that you used to be a quiet little thing who would never say boo to a goose.' She watched his retreating back and thought, crossly, it was only with you that I was quiet; no one else has ever accused me of being so.

Hero and Rufus, like their owners, were a well-matched pair. The ride was exhilarating for all concerned and when, one and a half hours later, they clattered back into the yard, they were all well pleased with the morning exercise. Over a late breakfast, Leo read *The Times* and Eleanor read her book. He glanced across, as he folded his paper, at her dark head bent intently over the pages.

'What are you reading so avidly, my dear?'

'A novel called, *Pride and Prejudice*. It is masterly; I can highly recommend it.' She grinned mischievously. 'You might find it worth studying.'

He twitched the book from her hand and flicked through it, his interest aroused by her remark. Eleanor watched his expression change to one of disgust. He frowned at her as he closed the book with a decided snap. 'I hope you are not suggesting that I am to become a pattern copy of that imbecile Darcy? He would not have lasted five minutes at the Battle of Talevera.'

'I should think that might be considered an

advantage in some circles,' she said, enjoying his disgruntlement.

'Would you prefer it if I was a town dandy and not a soldier, Ellie?'

She answered his question with one of her own. 'Would you prefer me if I was a docile debutante, Leo?'

'Heaven forefend,' he said, alarmed at the thought. 'I should die of *ennui* before a sennight had passed. At least married to you, my dear, my life will never be dull.'

Eleanor felt it only fair that she now answer his earlier question. 'And I would not like to be married to a tulip of the *ton*. At least we will have the exciting stories of your exploits to discuss after supper and will not be reduced to gossiping about the latest crim.con.'

'What do you know of that subject? I did not realize London gossip of that sort reached this far. Which reminds me, I heard from Gareth this morning. He, and my delightful sister-in-law Sophia, will be descending upon us the day after tomorrow.' He glared at Eleanor as if this was her fault. 'Though why they want to arrive three days before the wedding, I cannot imagine.'

'I hope they do not disapprove of me. The marchioness has the reputation for being very high in the instep. They might consider that the daughter of an impoverished gentleman no match for the youngest son of a duke.'

'Poppycock! It is no business of theirs who I choose to marry. They will have nothing to say on the matter, or they will have to answer to me,' Leo told her forcefully. 'You are not to worry Ellie. They will be delighted that I am finally getting shackled, after all, I am almost three and thirty.'

*   *   *

Eleanor tried not to worry about the forthcoming visit but she knew that Leo's illustrious relations would be bound to dislike her. She was not interested in domestic issues, or slavishly following fashion, and she would not be marrying at all if Aunt Prudence had left her any money of her own. To be a success in the *ton* a young lady had to make these things a priority. Eleanor believed she would never be able to do that; she believed that improving one's mind and improving the lot of those less fortunate than one's self was far more important than securing a husband and wearing the latest fashions.

8

Eleanor, leaving the ballroom to change for her daily ride with Leo could not help but notice that the housemaids and footmen were more visible than she was accustomed to.

She mentioned it to Leo as they trotted out of the yard. 'Leo, have you noticed the house appears to be in an uproar? Everyone is rushing around cleaning; did you instruct them to spring clean the house?'

He shook his head. 'Why should I have done so? I leave such matters to you; after all you are the mistress of the house now, aren't you?'

'I suppose I am. But I have given no instructions to anyone; indeed Mrs Basingstoke and Brown have not spoken to me since I returned several weeks ago.'

Even Leo, who had spent most of his adult life as a serving soldier, knew that etiquette had been severely breached. 'That is outrageous, Eleanor. Anything relating to the household should be discussed with you first. But it is you who has to ask to see the housekeeper; it is not her place to approach you first. I can scarcely believe you are

73

ignorant of this fact.'

She was stung by his disapproval. 'The house is obviously running smoothly without any interference from me. I thought you understood that I have no interest in things of that kind.'

'Then it is about time that you did, my girl. It is a woman's responsibility to run the house and supervise the children: it is the man's to see to everything else.'

'I have no idea how to order a house; I should just make a mull of it. It would be better to leave things as they are.'

'No, it would not. I will send Mrs Basingstoke to you and you must go through the accounts, the menus and discuss the arrangements for my brother's visit.' It was clear from his tone that there was to be no further argument on this point and Eleanor resigned herself to the dismal prospect of spending hours involved with things in which she had no interest. Her sigh must have been louder than she had intended.

'For God's sake, Ellie, grow up. Everyone has responsibilities and duties and I will not have you shirking yours. You have obviously been over-indulged, but that is going to stop.' He stared at her, holding Hero still, daring her to make a pert reply.

'Very well, I will do as you ask as I do not

have a choice.' She had begun to think they had reached an understanding but now the overbearing, intimidating stranger was back. For the first time since their rides had commenced she returned to the house feeling dispirited. Even the gallops and the hedges she had jumped had failed to cheer her. Leo's barked instruction, to be in the study within the hour, did not improve her mood.

Mary, as usual, greeted her cheerfully. 'I hope you enjoyed your ride, Miss Ellie.'

'No, I did not. I have to take over the running of the household, Mary. It is madness; I know nothing of such matters.'

'Well, I'm sure you will soon learn, I know it's not my place to criticize but it is not right that Mrs Basingstoke and Brown are making decisions without referring them to you. It's disrespectful to your position.'

Whilst in her bath, Eleanor considered the scolding she had received from Leo and began to see that, maybe, she had deserved it. The role of châtelaine was hers, whether she liked it or not.

Half an hour later she was waiting, as instructed, in the study for the housekeeper to appear. She had no idea what was expected of her; Leo, apart from ordering her to become the mistress of the house, had offered her no advice. She was an intelligent, well-educated and well-travelled young woman, what she didn't know she would soon learn.

★ ★ ★

The interview went far better than she could have hoped. The housekeeper, a pleasant outspoken woman, who knew just how things should be done, explained exactly what her future role was to be. She apologized for presuming to clean the house and start preparing the food for the coming celebration, but felt it wasn't her place to remind Eleanor of her duties.

'Thank you, Mrs Basingstoke, this has been a most informative meeting. I apologise most sincerely for not taking an interest sooner. In future things will be ordered as they should be,' Eleanor told her, sounding every inch the lady of the house.

'Now, Miss Eleanor, don't you worry. Everything is in hand and his lordship will have nothing to complain of, I promise you that.' She rose to leave. 'Will it be convenient to see you after breakfast tomorrow, Miss Eleanor?'

'Yes, that will be splendid. Good morning, and thank you for your help.' The study door opened again and she thought it was the housekeeper returning.

'Did you make your position clear, Eleanor?' Leo asked. 'Do the staff understand that all decisions pertaining to the household must go through you?'

'Yes, Leo, we have settled everything satisfactorily. But please try and remember this is a household and not a battalion of soldiers. It does not require to be ordered to perform; they are only too willing to do whatever is required.'

Leo was startled by her sharp rejoinder, but pleased she was taking her duties seriously. 'Point taken; I will leave everything in your capable hands. You have not disappointed me.'

She smiled. 'Odious creature, it is too late to wheedle round me now. I shall not forget the scold you gave me this morning; it quite ruined our ride.' He chuckled and they went into the dining-room for luncheon in complete accord.

★ ★ ★

The post-breakfast meeting with the house-keeper, the next day, went smoothly. Eleanor was now fully *au fait* with everything that had been arranged for the imminent arrival of their guests. When it was politely suggested that a conducted tour of the establishment, and an introduction to all household staff, might be appropriate she agreed. She wondered why this was necessary, as after all, she had known most of them since her arrival at Monk's Hall five years previously. The morning hung heavily before her; it left her far too much time to fret over the meeting with Leo's elder brother and his intimidating wife.

The intricacies of preserving table linen were beginning to pall when Eleanor thought she heard the sound of a carriage pulling up in front of the house. 'Pray excuse me, I do believe that our guests have arrived,' Eleanor interrupted the housekeeper's friendly monologue.

'My word, Miss Eleanor, you have sharp ears. We can easily continue this another time.'

Eleanor hurried back to her room to check her appearance was all it should be. Poking and peering in various cupboards might well have upset the extra effort Mary had made to turn her out well that morning.

Her maid was anxiously awaiting her return. 'Come on, miss, you will be wanted downstairs immediately. Let me straighten your hair and brush down your dress.'

The very modish, blue cambric muslin with a small check which Eleanor was wearing would pass muster anywhere. The matching blue sash, which tied at the side in two small bows with long floating ends, set off the outfit perfectly. Eleanor was glad that she had chosen a dress with long, closely fitting sleeves because she knew that wearing a shawl, whilst greeting guests, could be a recipe for disaster.

She was impatient to leave, for she quite definitely heard voices in the hall. 'I must go; it would be unpardonable to be late.'

'Off you go then; you look a picture, miss, if you don't mind my saying so.'

Eleanor sped from the room, but remembered, as she approached the stairs, to slow her pace to a more decorous walk. She had just started her ladylike descent when the strident tones of her future sister-in-law carried clearly from the hall.

'My dear, Leo, what a disaster! My heart goes out to you. To be forced to marry such a wild girl with no idea how to behave, I do declare we feel most strongly that the fortune attached to her will scarcely be enough to compensate.'

Eleanor was starting her retreat when Leo stepped forward. 'My love, there you are; come down and meet Gareth and Sophia; they have just this moment arrived.' He smiled warmly and walked up to meet her, keeping his back towards the visitors. He took her hands, squeezing them reassuringly, than bent to whisper in her ear, 'I warned you, sweetheart, but you would insist I asked my appalling sister-in-law.'

Eleanor's embarrassment evaporated and she giggled. 'Hush, Leo, they might hear you.'

He was unrepentant. 'She is infamous for her lack of tact, Ellie, and you must disregard anything she says. As I told you before, it is my business who I choose to marry and I have chosen you.' He turned and, slipping her arm through his, led her down the stairs. The marchioness, having been comprehensively snubbed by her brother-in-law, was rigid with anger beside her more equable spouse.

'Gareth, allow me to present my betrothed, Miss Eleanor Walters.' Eleanor offered her hand and curtsied gracefully to the tall, elegant man watching her through amused, pale-blue eyes. The marquis took her hand and, raising it to his lips, bowed formally.

'I am delighted to meet you at last, Miss Walters. Leo has mentioned you to us many times, over the years.'

Eleanor glanced sideways at her fiancé, smiling urbanely beside her. She could easily imagine what he had said, remembering only too vividly the unflattering remarks she had overheard three years ago.

Gareth, still holding her hand, drew her towards his wife. Sophia, Eleanor could see, was still slender, her three pregnancies not having thickened her figure one jot. The corn-coloured hair framed a classic, heart-shaped face which, if only she would smile more often would be truly lovely.

'Sophia, my dear, allow me to present Miss Eleanor Walters to you,' Gareth drawled, enjoying his wife's discomfiture. Much as he loved her, he was not blind to her faults, and it wasn't often she received such a resounding set down.

Sophia, every inch the duchess-in-waiting, inclined her head slightly, and raked Eleanor from top to toe with a gimlet stare. Her intention had been to comment unfavourably on her future sister-in-law's attire, but found, to her surprise, she was unable to find fault with Eleanor's appearance.

Surprise softened her expression and the greeting was almost friendly. 'I am pleased to meet you, Miss Walters. And, I must ask, where did you acquire such a delightful gown? It is quite out of the ordinary way, you know.'

Eleanor's curtsy was far deeper than she had intended; the unexpected compliment disarming her. She straightened and discovered that she was not so much taller than

Sophia; indeed they were of a startlingly, similar build. She looked again at the marquis and realized that he was almost as tall as Leo, although less muscular, but there was no doubting their fraternity.

She stared openly from one to the other, much to their combined amusement. She turned accusingly to Leo. 'Leo, why did you not tell me your brother is a pattern copy of you?'

Leo laughed; his unconventional betrothed had not disappointed him. 'Ellie, sweetheart, I think you will find that, as the younger brother, it is more correct to say I am — '

She interrupted him laughing, 'Please do not pick words with me, Leo, for you know exactly what I meant.' If the outspoken reply shocked their guests they were far too polite to comment.

Leo, who preferred plain speaking, answered in kind. 'That my brother and I could pass as twins has been remarked upon before. But I think you will find, my dear, that the resemblance is on the outside only.'

Ellie laughed aloud. 'I am delighted to hear you say so, my lord, for I am finding that dealing with one of you is more than enough.' Still smiling, she turned back to the waiting marchioness, who did not know whether to be scandalized or amused by the brisk exchange between Upminster and his betrothed.

'My lady,' Eleanor began, 'you asked me a moment ago where I got my gown. I am so pleased that you admire it, as I designed it myself.'

'But it is completely *à la mode*; I can hardly believe my eyes.' Sophia stepped up to examine the dress, but even under such close scrutiny she could find no fault. 'It is perfectly done, my dear. I could only wish my own modiste was able to cut and finish as well.'

Eleanor, delighted that cordial relations had been established, and more than ready to forget Sophia's earlier comments, took her arm impulsively. 'Would you like to come and see my workshop? I have set up the ballroom and have several girls sewing my bride clothes.' She paused, suddenly remembering her new position. 'I must apologize; I should have asked if you would like to go to your rooms to refresh yourselves after your journey. The housekeeper will show you the way.' Mrs Basingstoke was waiting patiently at the foot of the stairs, ready to take them up.

Sophia smiled, deciding after all that she rather liked Eleanor's unconventional manners. 'Later, Eleanor — I may call you

Eleanor, I hope, after all we are to be sisters soon? — I am too eager to see how your trousseau is being assembled.'

Eleanor turned to the housekeeper. 'Thank you, Mrs Basingstoke; if you would see that the trunks are taken up, that will be all for now.' Leo nodded approvingly; pleased she had remembered her duties. 'Would you like some refreshment now, or will you wait until luncheon is served?' She addressed this question to both the marquis and his wife.

Gareth bowed politely and refused the offer saying that he had much to discuss with his brother before they ate. Satisfied she had done all she should, Eleanor led the way across the great hall and in to the ballroom, now unrecognizable as a place of entertainment.

Girls sat sewing industriously at trestles with Mary supervising their work. The spindly gilt chairs that had lined the walls were grouped together and festooned with a kaleidoscope of colourful materials. Bolts of satin, silk, cotton, damask and muslin spilt across them, giving the huge room the brilliance of an Indian bazaar.

Sophia recognized quality when she saw it. If materials like these were to be placed in a London emporium they would be snapped up in seconds. 'My dear child, wherever did you get all these wonderful fabrics?' She ran a particularly rich, gold figured silk through her fingers. 'This is exquisite; I have never seen anything quite like this for sale in London.'

'It is Indian; my aunt and I chose it when we were there. If you would like it, my lady, please accept it as a gift. I have more than enough for my needs.'

'Eleanor, I could not possibly accept such a generous gift. You can have no idea of the value of this material.'

Eleanor insisted. 'It cost very little in Delhi, my lady, whatever it is worth over here. I would like you to have it.' She thought for a moment, seeing the marchioness was still unwilling to accept the material. 'I know, it can be your Christmas gift from Leo and me, but you can have it early.'

'Oh very well, child, I can hardly refuse a Christmas gift, can I? And, my dear, please call me Sophia, I am not one to stand on formality.' If her husband had heard this remark he would have fallen from his chair in shock.

The sound of the luncheon gong prevented Eleanor from showing Sophia anything else but they agreed to return as soon as the meal was over. The two ladies returned to the hall chatting happily, like a pair of bosom bows.

Leo turned to his brother and said quietly,

'That is a guinea you owe me; I told you how it would be and I am right.'

'You have found a veritable treasure, Leo. Anyone who can win my Sophia's friendship so soon is nothing short of a miracle worker. I must admit that I had my reservations about this marriage but they are gone now. You have my full approval, Leo, not that you need it.'

'No, Gareth, I do not,' Leo replied, 'but I am sure Ellie will be relieved; she is eager to be accepted and was worried.'

'I think she is delightful, and we can safely say that my wife would now agree with me. You must spend Christmas and New Year with us; Eleanor needs to meet the duke and the rest of the family.'

Eleanor strolled over to join them, pleased the morning had gone so well, after such an inauspicious start. She took Leo's proffered arm and they led the way into the small dining-room. She spoke softly, not wishing to be overheard. 'Sophia is not half as bad as I feared, after all, and I really like your brother.'

Leo raised a quizzical eyebrow. 'I am delighted to hear that, my love, as we have been invited to spend Christmas and New Year with them and it would have been unfortunate if you were still at daggers drawn with Sophia.'

The sound of their mingled laughter

rippled round the dining-room causing Brown, a stickler for convention, to frown disapprovingly. Such levity was unseemly, and standards of behaviour, he considered, were not being maintained. He looked to the marquis and marchioness, expecting to see his sentiments reciprocated. He was disappointed; both were smiling their approval, glad that Leo and Eleanor's relationship appeared to be a love match, when they had feared it could, in the circumstances, be no more than a marriage of convenience.

9

Eleanor went down for breakfast the following morning expecting to find Leo on his own. In her limited experience, the *ton* were rarely seen before noon. Morning calls that were made at three in the afternoon had always seemed absurd to her.

'Good morning, my lords,' she said, smiling, and dropped a curtsy, as they both stood up politely and half bowed. 'I did not expect to see you down so early, Gareth; I hope your room was not uncomfortable.'

'My room is perfect, Eleanor, thank you, but you will not see Sophia until noon,' he replied. They sat down, Eleanor having chosen coddled eggs and toast.

When they were private she looked across. 'Leo, I am worried about Rufus. John attempted to lunge him and it was a disaster. As I cannot ride him at the moment I am at a loss to know how to proceed.' Her comments were intended to provoke Leo into rescinding his instructions but his solution was quite different.

'I will take him out this morning and Gareth can ride Hero,' he told her, and waited for her protest.

Eleanor was quiet for a moment, her expression thoughtful. 'Thank you, Leo, that seems a sensible idea.' She returned to her breakfast and no more was said on that particular subject. Eleanor was fuming silently at Leo's highhanded assumption that he could ride her horse without permission. But she was determined not to embarrass the marquis with one of her outbursts.

Arguing in private with one's intended was, she considered, perfectly acceptable; to do it in public was not. She hoped that Rufus would have the good sense to toss his rider into a ditch at the first opportunity and literally bring him down to earth with a bump.

When the party reassembled at noon, for luncheon, Eleanor was disappointed to hear the ride had gone splendidly. 'That stallion of yours, Eleanor, is a champion. With me on board, this morning, Hero was unable to keep up,' Leo informed her, seemingly unaware how his words offended her. 'I think it would be better if I got you a more suitable hack and rode Rufus myself from now on.'

She had heard enough. With exaggerated care she pushed back her chair and stood up, shaking with rage. 'How dare you,' she said, her voice low and dripping with dislike.

Ignoring the shocked expressions of her guests, she continued, for it was far too late to think about their sensibilities. 'Rufus is my horse. I only agreed that you should ride him this morning because I had no wish to argue the point in public. You will not ride him again and I will not ride another horse.'

Leo spoke quietly, but his words carried the authority of command. 'Sit down, Eleanor, you are embarrassing our guests.' His grey eyes held hers in a freezing stare. She hesitated for a second, then common sense prevailed and she sat, her face pale, her hands clenched under the table in anger. Having achieved his objective, Leo turned the subject to more general, safer topics. But Eleanor ate nothing more. She answered any comments directed to her but took no further part in the conversation.

When the interminable meal was over she walked swiftly from the room, leaving the others in no doubt of her extreme displeasure. Leo smiled coolly at his guests. 'Please excuse me; I have to speak to Eleanor in private. I am sure you will understand.' And he strode out of the room his grim expression boding ill for Eleanor when he found her.

★　★　★

She, meanwhile, had headed out to the stables wanting to reassure herself that Rufus was still her horse, that he hadn't changed his allegiance to the hated usurper. The yard was quiet, the grooms and stable boys elsewhere. Rufus, recognizing his mistress, whinnied a greeting and stamped in excitement.

She ran over to him, unbolted the loose-box door and slipped inside. Her anger evaporated as she rested her burning cheek against his neck. Instead desolation overwhelmed her; she had disgraced herself, embarrassed her guests and angered Leo and for what purpose? Whatever she said Leo could do as he pleased, for he was her legal guardian and in two days' time would be her husband, and he had absolute control over her person and her property.

She let the scalding tears flow down her face and the giant stallion stood still, supporting her despair, sensing that his special human needed him. It was here that Leo found her. The sound of her sobbing could be heard clearly coming from inside the stable. He paused outside the box, finding his justifiable fury beginning to soften at the sound of her misery.

He quietly unlocked the door and went in. Eleanor sensing his intrusion stiffened. Her fear instantly communicated itself to Rufus and he flattened his ears and curled back his lips in anger. Before either of them could react he half reared, and screamed his anger at the man who had frightened his owner. He lunged at Leo, sinking his teeth into his shoulder, pinning him against the wall with his enormous weight.

Eleanor shouted, her unhappiness and fear forgotten, in her horror. 'Rufus, let go of him. Let him go, now.' She grabbed his halter and pulled hard but Rufus was too enraged to allow someone as small as her to shift him. Leo, his chest slowly crushing beneath the weight, remained calm.

He raised his free hand and placed it on Rufus's long nose and spoke softly, persuasively, breathing his words into the horse's flared nostrils.

'All right old boy. Calm down. Relax, Rufus; I am not going to hurt her.' He kept repeating the words and Rufus listened. His ears flicked forward and he stepped back releasing Leo's shoulder as he did so. Leo remained flat against the wall and the horse lowered his head and nudged him gently, as if in an apology.

John and the two stable boys had heard the commotion and arrived in the yard as Leo slowly slid down the wall to end in an undignified heap on the floor.

'Oh, Leo, what have I done?' Eleanor dropped to her knees to cradle his unresisting head in her lap. She stroked the dark, sweat-stained hair from his forehead and stared, appalled, at the unconscious man lying, ghostlike, in her arms. The box door was flung open and the anxious face of the head groom appeared. 'Fetch help, John. Fetch the marquis from the Hall. His lordship has been injured,' Eleanor ordered, striving to keep the panic she was feeling out of her voice.

Leo lay silent, his breathing, to her ears, sounded harsh and laboured. 'Please, Leo, do not die, how could I bear it if you died?' she whispered, fresh tears springing from her eyes. As she spoke the words out loud an astounding truth became apparent. She looked down at the man in her arms. Somehow, over the days, her dislike and distrust had turned into a deep, abiding, irrevocable love. Her tears dripped unheeded on to Leo's face. 'Oh God,' she prayed, 'I beg you, please do not let him die.'

One grey eye flickered open, quickly followed by the other. They crinkled slightly at the corners as he grinned up at her. 'I have absolutely no intention of turning up my toes, my angel, so you can stop crying and help me up.'

The radiance of her smile transformed her face. 'I am so sorry, Leo, I did not mean to, but you must lie still until Gareth comes,' she babbled, too relieved to care that she was talking nonsense. She heard the sound of pounding feet and the marquis arrived at the box entrance.

Leo extended his uninjured arm to his brother. 'Help me up, Gareth, but go carefully, I think I might have cracked a couple of ribs,' he told him cheerfully, his colour almost fully restored.

Gareth grabbed Leo's arm and, bracing himself against the door frame, slowly returned him to his feet. 'Good God, Leo, what happened here? Did that blasted animal attack you?' He glared angrily at the very subdued chestnut standing quietly at the far end of his stable.

Eleanor was about to tell Gareth that he was right when Leo prevented her. He balanced himself precariously against the wall and smiling, he offered her his hand. She took it and, mesmerized by the compelling gleam in his eyes, she stepped unquestion-ingly into the shelter of his arm, her reply left unspoken.

Leo held her close, hoping to demonstrate to her that he was not seriously hurt. 'Ellie love, do not look so wretched; I am a soldier,

94

remember? It takes more than an angry horse to stop me.'

She wiped her eyes on his shoulder and sniffed. 'You scared me, Leo. You were so white and still that I thought you were dying and it would have been my fault.'

He squeezed her shoulder to emphasize his reply. 'Do not be stupid. What happened was entirely my responsibility.'

The marquis wanted to know what had occurred. 'What happened, Leo? Why were you attacked?'

Leo's expression was rueful. 'Rufus was protecting Ellie; he sensed my anger and reacted as one would expect. It serves me right. No blame for this incident belongs to the horse' — he smiled at Ellie, still in his embrace — 'or to you, sweetheart, it was entirely my fault.'

Eleanor stood on tiptoes and placed a feather-light kiss on his cheek, then quickly stepped away, not certain that even in his present state he wouldn't reciprocate. 'You will need a doctor. I will send John immediately to fetch him from the village.'

'No need; Sam can sort me out. He knows more about broken bones than any quack I have ever met. Right, Gareth, I think I am ready to stagger back to the house but I will need your support, as well as John's, I fear.'

'You have it always, Leo, you know that,' the marquis replied.

Eleanor led the way back, listening with distress to the strangled groans coming from behind her as Leo was slowly assisted along the path. Sam, Leo's manservant who had accompanied him from the Peninsular to Waterloo, was waiting at the side entrance. He immediately took charge and within a short time, and with a minimum of fuss, the injured man was deposited on his bed upstairs. Eleanor's tentative offer of help was firmly dismissed and she was forced, reluctantly, to return to the drawing-room and the censure of her guests.

Sophia had fully intended to ring a peal over Eleanor, but on seeing her wan and bedraggled appearance relented, which surprised both herself and her husband, who had just joined them.

Instead she was sympathetic and supportive, a role she was unused to playing. 'Do come and sit down, my dear girl, you look quite done in.' She steered Ellie to a *chaise-longue* and gently pushed her down. 'There, lie back, put up your feet and I will ring for some refreshment.'

The sight of the straw and horse dung sticking to Ellie's slippers almost threw her but she steadied and continued kindly, 'What a terrible thing to have happened. But it could have been so much worse, you know.'

Eleanor looked at her dumbly, unable to think of anything sensible to say. Of course it could have been worse, Leo could have been killed. Her face crumpled at the thought and fresh tears filled her eyes. 'Oh, I am so sorry; I am not usually such a watering pot.'

Sophia dug into a commodious reticule and removed a dainty embroidered square. Her husband laughed and offered his own handkerchief instead. 'Take this one, my dear; you look as though you will need it.'

Slowly Eleanor recovered her composure and soon she was able to speak coherently. She cleared her throat experimentally. Two pairs of eyes were, at once, focused on her. She smiled warmly at her captive audience. 'Well, there is one good thing about Leo's accident.' She paused and wondered if what she was thinking was better left unsaid.

'Go on, Eleanor, please continue,' Gareth prompted, interested to hear how a positive gloss could be put on the events of the afternoon.

She felt she had no option but to continue. 'At least Leo is no longer angry with me. He is truly terrifying when he is enraged, you know.' Sophia and Gareth looked at her, then at each other, and laughed out loud.

'Eleanor, my dear, you are incorrigible.' Gareth told her, still chuckling. 'I honestly believe my brother is finally well matched. You will make him a perfect, if unconventional, wife.'

Eleanor blushed under his approving gaze, not sure why her statement had caused them both such merriment. A knock at the door heralded the arrival of Sam with news of Leo.

'His lordship begs to tell you that he will be down for dinner tonight. He has a nasty gash on his right shoulder and several bruised ribs, but nothing broken. He has had a lot worse and still fought alongside his men, so a few bruises don't bother him.'

*   *   *

While Eleanor lay on her bed her mind was in turmoil. Loving Leo, she believed, made everything so much more complicated. It would be harder not to respond to his overtures now her emotions were engaged. She knew — for hadn't he told her so himself? — that a man could desire a woman without loving her. She tossed restlessly from side to side, trying to decide if she would prefer a marriage in name only to a consummated relationship when there was love on only one side.

There were only thirty-six hours before her marriage, and she had to make a decision before the ceremony. If she wanted a real relationship it was only fair to indicate to Leo that she had changed her mind.

When Mary arrived to help her dress for dinner she found her mistress suffering from a sick headache and far too unwell to go down. Eleanor's apologies were conveyed at once to Brown who was charged with delivering them to Lord Upminster when he came down. Her megrim was so severe Eleanor was unable to rise the next day either. The night before her wedding she finally slept, exhausted by the pain and nausea, too poorly to worry about anything at all.

· 10

'What time is it, Mary?' Eleanor asked, as her abigail drew back the heavy blue curtain letting in the morning light.

'Only just gone eight o'clock, miss, you have plenty of time before you need to get up.' Mary picked up the tray she had placed on the side table and brought it over. 'Toast and tea, nothing more, until we see if you can keep this down.'

'My headache has gone completely and the nausea too. I am not very hungry but think I can manage to eat a little dry toast.' Although Eleanor's face was pale and drawn, her eyes were clear and she felt well enough to face the coming ordeal. 'I will have my bath early, I think, as I need to leave time for my hair to dry.'

'At nine o'clock then? That will leave two hours before you need to be downstairs.'

'Thank you, Mary, nine o'clock will do perfectly. I hope his lordship likes my wedding gown; it is very plain.'

'Not plain, miss; it is elegant and stylish. That heavy cream silk brocade you chose does not need any fancy flounces and bows.'

Left alone, Eleanor sipped her tea, pensively, and stared at the simple silk dress hanging on the rail at the far side of her chamber, still unsure if her design was grand enough for such an important occasion.

A tap on the door interrupted her thoughts. As Mary had been sent away she realized she must answer the summons herself. She slipped out of bed, hastily pulled on her robe, and walked over to the door. Cautiously she opened it a crack, not sure who she might find waiting there.

'Eleanor, child, whatever are you doing?' Sophia entered quickly. 'Where is your girl? She should be here to open the door; it is not your job.'

'I sent Mary to have breakfast, Sophia.' It seemed a little late to invite her visitor in as she was already at the rail examining the gown.

'This is lovely, my dear. The material is exquisite, the cut superb. It is exactly right.'

'My wish is to show Leo that he is not marrying a child. He appears to be rather confused on that subject.'

'In that case you will succeed. Not even Leo could imagine you were anything but a fully grown woman in this.'

Eleanor was delighted. 'I am so glad you approve. I was worried it was too simple for a wedding dress.'

'Leo will love it, I am certain of that,' Sophia answered smiling. 'Now return to bed, Eleanor, for I want to talk to you.'

Eleanor, guessing what kind of talk Sophia was probably referring to, skipped hastily back under the covers. Sophia pulled up a dainty padded chair and sat beside her.

'Leo has been beside himself with anxiety; it was all we could do to stop him visiting your bedchamber.'

'I am glad you did; I have cast up my accounts in front of him once and I would have hated to have done so a second time,' Eleanor replied with a rueful smile.

'It was most improper of him to wish to visit you in here, but it does demonstrate his interest in your well-being.' Sophia broke off for a moment, wishing to choose her next words carefully. 'I understand that you wish your marriage to be in name only, is that correct?' Eleanor nodded, blushing slightly.

'Do you still hold the same point of view, my dear? I cannot help noticing that your feelings now seem to be engaged and wondered if you could possibly have changed your mind.'

This was exactly what Eleanor had done. It was trying to make this decision that had, she believed, caused her horrible headache. 'Although I have changed my mind, Sophia, I am not yet ready to become a true wife. You see, although I have been acquainted with Leo since I was fourteen years old, and first came to live here, it is only since my return from India that I have begun to know him properly.'

'Quite so, my dear, I fully understand. A few weeks are not nearly long enough for an engagement. If circumstances were different you would have had several months to get to know each other better before your wedding.'

'I know almost nothing about Leo,' Eleanor told her, 'apart from the fact that he was a Colonel in the infantry and a hero at Waterloo.'

Sophia nodded. 'Well, I can tell you about his youth, if you would like to hear it?'

'Of course I would. There is one thing that puzzles me and that is why he has no money of his own. Surely His Grace, the Duke of Rothmere, is a very wealthy man?'

'You are correct in that assumption. His father is one of the warmest men in England. Let me explain. Gareth was scarcely four years old when Leo was born and their poor mama died soon after the birth.'

'How dreadful!' Eleanor was deeply saddened by the thought of the two little boys left motherless.

'The duke,' Sophia continued, 'blamed Leo

for her death and never forgave him. He was ignored, or mistreated, by his father and the only affection he received came from Gareth.'

'So that is why he became a soldier so young, to get away from home. But how could he afford a commission if he had no money of his own?'

'His grandmama, the dowager duchess, who was still alive then, paid for it; her small legacy, and his half pay as a colonel, are the only funds he has.'

'I believe that he is to resign after we are wed and devote himself to running the estate. There is much to do: it has been sadly neglected since Uncle Joseph passed away. I am afraid that Aunt Prudence had no interest in such matters.' The sound of a bath being filled in the dressing-room next door reminded them of the time.

Sophia rose to go. 'I will let Gareth know straightaway your feelings on the subject of your marriage, and then he can inform Leo. I am certain he will be content to wait until you are better acquainted.' She smiled benevolently at Eleanor. 'It is a profound relief to me that I do not have to discuss what happens in the marriage bed just yet; time enough to explain everything when you visit us at Christmas.'

Eleanor giggled. 'Sophia, I know all about

what happens between a man and a woman. One would have to have been blind not to see when it was demonstrated so openly in some of the places we visited.'

She swung her legs out of bed and grinned at Sophia's shocked countenance. 'I must admit that I could not see why anyone could possibly wish to engage in such a strange, and uncomfortable-looking, pastime. However, since I met Leo again I am beginning to see that maybe I was wrong.'

'Eleanor, my dear, you should not talk of such things, even to me. I honestly think that too much travel is not a good thing for a gently bred young lady.' Sophia said, shocked by what she had heard.

Mary came quietly into the room to indicate that the bath was ready. 'I will see you downstairs at eleven o'clock, Eleanor. And you must not worry; I am sure you will never regret marrying Leo. He will make you very happy.'

'I do hope so, but sometimes I wonder. I know that he is intelligent, handsome, charming, kind and brave, but he is also arrogant, overbearing and has the worst temper of anyone I have ever met.' As she listed his good and bad points she realized that her doubts had made her speak more forcefully that she had intended.

'I admit that he is no paragon, but like his brother, my dear Gareth, he will make you an excellent husband. His rough edges will wear away; just give him time.' With these last words Sophia swept regally from the room, her mission accomplished, happy that Leo would get the answer he desired.

★ ★ ★

After a leisurely bath, Eleanor sat in front of the fire, her hair swirling like a shiny brown waterfall about her shoulders, whilst her maid rubbed it dry. At a few minutes to eleven she was dressed and stood in front of the full-length glass fascinated by her own reflection. Her height, her slenderness and her swan-like neck were all enhanced by the dress. Mary had arranged her hair in a coronet, allowing a few stray curls to escape on either side of her oval face.

Eleanor smiled at her reflection. She spun round slowly, the dress following her every movement, enjoying the feeling of confidence that it gave. 'I am ready to go down. This is one occasion that I will not keep his lordship waiting.'

Leo was indeed waiting, with growing impatience, in the great hall below. He was resplendent in his full regimentals. The short, scarlet coat emphasized his broad shoulders, and the heavy gold frogging added to his splendour. His tightly fitting buckskins and black polished Hessians completed the ensemble. He looked superb.

Gareth, dressed in a blue superfine tailed coat, and gold-embroidered waistcoat, with tightly fitting beige pantaloons, was smart, but no match for his brother. Sophia, in a gown of cherry-red worsted, with a matching pelisse, and a bonnet that Gareth had rudely described as 'looking exactly like a bright red coal scuttle covered in fruit' was dressed in what could only be called 'the first stare of fashion.'

Leo looked around when he heard the sound of footsteps coming lightly along the upstairs corridor. He marched swiftly to his place at the foot of the stairs, ready to greet his bride. At the sight of the beautiful young woman floating towards him he was struck silent. He found his voice at last.

'I must be the luckiest man in Christendom,' he said quietly, his eyes never leaving hers, 'to be marrying such a vision of loveliness.' He offered her his arm and she placed a trembling hand upon it, grateful for the support it gave. Her fingers closed involuntarily and she could feel the muscular strength beneath the cloth.

Leo led her out to the waiting carriage and handed her in. Mary rushed forward and carefully arranged the dress to avoid it creasing during the short ride to church. The marquis and marchioness travelled in their own carriage behind the bridal pair.

'That dress is stunning, Ellie, my sweet, you have surpassed yourself.' Leo told her, unable to drag his eyes away.

'Thank you, Leo, I am glad that you like it,' she replied, carefully controlling her voice, trying to disguise the growing tension she felt sitting so close to him. The fabric of her gown, and his buckskins, were the only barrier between them. Eleanor tried, unsuccessfully, to ease her thigh away from his, sure the heat generated by their touch must, by now, be flooding her face with tell-tale pink.

He took her gloved hands in his just as the carriage lurched to a stop. 'You will not regret this marriage, Ellie, I promise you. I will try and control my foul temper and behave as a member of the *ton*.' She returned the gentle pressure of his fingers, overcome by his promise to try and reform his ways, for her.

She smiled shyly. 'And I promise that I will try my best to conform and to behave as I know I should.'

'A pact then, little bird,' Leo said quietly, and he raised her hands to his lips and kissed, first the tips and then, turning them over, each palm. His gentle touch sent tremors around her overheated body.

The footman, who had accompanied them on the box, opened the carriage door. The steps were let down. The moment had come. The marriage of Miss Eleanor Walters to Colonel, Lord Leo Upminster, was about to take place.

The church seemed dark and unwelcoming and the vicar nervous. Even the vases of flowers placed around the church, especially for the occasion, failed to make it inviting. Lord Upminster led his bride to the altar and, in the presence of God, they exchanged their vows.

Afterwards, when Leo spoke her name she glanced up, startled, hardly able to comprehend that she was now a wife, a member of the aristocracy and no longer plain Miss Walters but Lady Upminster.

'I believe, at this point, sweetheart, I am allowed to kiss the bride.' His voice was light and teasing. She blushed and her lips parted expectantly. Although the kiss was brief it left her breathless and she clung on to his coat, fearing she might fall.

'Congratulations, Leo and Eleanor,' Gareth said. 'May I be permitted to embrace my new sister?'

Reluctantly, Leo released his bride and stepped aside allowing his brother to take her in his arms and place a chaste kiss on her cheek. Next Sophia hugged Eleanor tight and whispered that all was well and that Leo had been told.

The wedding party left the church and returned to the waiting carriages. On the return journey, Leo sat, face sombre and pensive, his long legs outstretched and Eleanor's hand still held firmly in his. 'Eleanor, do you realize you have just placed your life in the hands of a man as ill suited to married life as any you are likely to meet?'

'I am sure you are no more unsuited to marriage than any bachelor of your age,' she said soothingly. 'It is only natural that you should feel some qualms, but I promise to try not to be a burden to you. I will not require you to be dancing attendance on me all the time.' She stopped, arrested by the expression on his face. He was looking at her as though she had run mad.

He smiled, shaking his head as he spoke. 'Do you think I am concerned about my adjustment? No, Ellie, it is you I am thinking of. Do you realize that being married means you are no longer independent, you are my wife, answerable to me for everything you do? It is my duty to protect and advise you, as it is yours to behave as you should and do as you are told.' This last statement was spoken with a decided glint in his eye. Eleanor's protest died unspoken.

She smiled. 'I have promised to try and behave and you have promised not to lose your temper, which is a good start, surely?' She leant her head, trustingly, against his shoulder, and needing no further encouragement, Leo released her hand and encircled her shoulder, pulling her even closer.

'Look at me,' he urged, his voice heavy with passion. Obediently she raised her head and felt herself being devoured by his hunger. 'Darling, I know you want to wait, but you can see how much I desire you and I believe that you feel the same way too.' As his mouth closed over hers she felt her reservations being crushed under the power of his passion. How could she deny him what he wanted when she loved him, and believed she wanted it too?

11

The marquis and marchioness departed immediately after the wedding breakfast leaving Eleanor and Leo to spend the afternoon together. The coach was barely out of sight before Eleanor caught hold of Leo's sleeve.

'Can I ride now Sophia and Gareth have gone, Leo?'

'Only if I accompany you, remember.'

'Please come; I am sure you would enjoy a gallop across the park as much as I would.'

'You are right, I would.' He glanced up at the sun, already low on the horizon. 'We have only an hour or so of daylight left so, if we are to ride, it had better be now.'

'I have to take off this dress but will be back down in ten minutes.'

Leo smiled wickedly. 'As I also have to come upstairs would you like me to assist you in any way, my love?'

'No, Mary and I will manage, but thank you for your kind offer.' She blushed and sped up the stairs to her chamber before he could embarrass her further. In spite of her haste he was beside her as she reached the door. He blocked her path; his broad shoulders appearing to fill the entrance.

'I am your husband now, Ellie; you must not bolt every time I tease you.' He brushed his fingers lightly across her face. She tried to find an answer that would not sound silly but her brain refused to work and no words came. Leo was sapping her strength to resist.

Hardly aware she was moving she closed the gap between them and stepped in to his embrace, her arms encircling his neck. His arms locked behind her and he leant back, lifting her from her feet, as he kissed her passionately.

After several minutes Leo pushed her away gently with a shaky sigh. 'I think that is enough for now, my love, or it will be dark before we reach the stables.' He scanned her face and satisfied with what he saw there, kissed her once more, hard, on her swollen lips and strode off to his own room. 'Be downstairs in ten minutes, Ellie, or I will leave without you.'

Eleanor entered her bedchamber and was pleased to find Mary waiting there, her new riding habit already out. Ten minutes, to the second, later she was downstairs to meet her husband.

'I am impressed,' he said grinning, 'A punctual wife is a novelty. I have only been here two minutes myself.'

'Do not sound so smug, you had far less to remove than I did, or I would have been here sooner.'

'I did offer to help you, remember, but you unkindly refused.' He was openly laughing now, enjoying her growing annoyance at his teasing.

'Oh do be quiet, Leo. You are being deliberately provocative,' she said rudely and marched off, back straight, head high, trying to ignore his chuckles as he followed her down the passage.

'Now, now, Eleanor; it was only this morning that you promised to honour and obey me, and already you have broken your vows.'

'They will not be the only thing I break,' she threatened, intending to sound cross.

'Baggage,' he replied affectionately. 'I can see you are going to run me ragged and I shall decline into a sad and brow-beaten man, a shadow of my former self.'

'Lord Upminster, you are an idiot, and I am only surprised no one has told you so before.' The smile she gave him quite took his breath away.

He pulled her hand through his arm, drawing her close. 'Do you know,' he said pleasantly, 'I believe no one else has ever had the temerity to address me so disrespectfully.'

She struggled to remove his hand but Leo's grip was unyielding. 'Do you wish me to apologize?' she asked, her voice reflecting the fear that her teasing had truly offended him.

'Apologize?' he murmured thoughtfully. 'No, I had been thinking more of a penalty to be paid for every insult.'

'Penalty? What sort of penalty? I would much rather apologize, you know, Leo.'

'I have not yet decided. But I promise you will be the first to know when I do, my sweet.' He reached out and gripped her chin, turning her face to his. His expression changed, instantly, to concern when he saw the fear in her eyes.

'God damn it!' he swore, disgusted with himself. 'I was teasing you, little one; please do not look so scared, I had not meant to upset you.' He pulled her into his arms and held her, cupping the back of her head and pressing her face protectively into his shoulder. Slowly the tension left her body, she relaxed into his warmth, feeling a little foolish at her overreaction.

★　★　★

Eleanor changed again for dinner, choosing a yellow damask day dress, the most demure she owned. The memory of the two passionate exchanges, one in the carriage on the return from the church and the other outside her bedroom door, had frightened her by their intensity.

She was not sure she was ready to become a full wife and was regretting having encouraged him by her responses. She hoped her choice of gown would indicate to him how she felt because she knew she could never discuss such an intimate subject with a man, husband or not.

Leo had changed into a black evening coat, a snowy white, elaborate cravat and a grey silk waistcoat and black pantaloons. Eleanor refused the sherry he offered and sat stiffly on the edge of a chair, mute with embarrassment in front of the overwhelming presence of the man in black evening dress.

It was a relief to both of them when dinner was announced. Leo offered her his arm and they walked sedately through to the small dining-room. Eleanor could feel the carefully leashed power in Leo's arm and her heart missed a beat and she swallowed nervously. Bravely, she risked a glance at his face and saw his expression was serious and remote.

Dinner was torture for Eleanor. She was incapable of finding anything sensible to say and was able to reply to all Leo's conversational overtures with only one word answers. In the end he gave up the attempt to involve her and the meal was completed in near silence. As the final covers were removed Leo spoke, his voice sounding unnaturally loud after the prolonged hush.

'I will not join you for tea, Eleanor. I have business to attend to in the study.' He stared at her pale face, all signs of the happy carefree girl, he had teased earlier, had disappeared. 'I have to go to London tomorrow to see the lawyers, and sign all the papers relating to the inheritance.' He waited, expecting some kind of response.

'Yes, I understand. Will you be gone for long?' She couldn't help hoping his absence would not be short.

'Several weeks, I am afraid. I have also to visit Horse Guards and resign my commission. I should definitely be back in time to leave for our visit.'

'What about Rufus? Can I ride when you are away, if John accompanies me?'

Leo nodded. 'Yes, you can. Also, if there any changes you wish to make here, in my absence, please feel free to do so. I want you to be happy, Eleanor, and have no wish to stint you in any way.'

'Thank you, Leo. There are one or two

things I would like to do. Is there a budget I must follow?'

'You may spend whatever you need, within reason of course. I know you are not extravagant and will not waste money unnecessarily.' He leaned over the table and took her cold hands in his. 'I think I know what is troubling you, Ellie; you wish me to give you more time before making you my true wife?' His eyes were kind and his words gentle.

'Leo, I know I have encouraged you to believe that I was ready but I find, now the time has come, that I am not. I am truly sorry.'

He released her hands and stood up. 'You do not have to apologize, my love, I was a brute to try and force the issue.' Unexpectedly he smiled, transforming his face, making him seem younger and more approachable. 'That is the real reason I am going away tomorrow. I cannot trust myself to stay out of your bed if I am here; I want you as my wife and I am finding it almost impossible to wait.'

Eleanor jumped up impulsively and ran round the table to fling herself into his arms, perhaps not the wisest course to follow after Leo's admission. 'Thank you, I knew you would understand. I promise I will not keep you waiting any longer than I have to.'

Finding the woman he wanted so desperately back in his arms tested Leo's iron control to the limit. He stepped out of her embrace so subtly she was unaware she had been rejected.

'I suggest you retire now, Ellie, it has been a long, exciting day.' He held her by the shoulders for a moment longer then removed his hands. 'I will be gone before you rise tomorrow so I will say farewell now.' He tipped her face and kissed her gently. 'Please try and behave yourself whilst I am away, and if you need me, my man will fetch me at once.'

'Goodbye, Leo, I will miss you; take care and please do not overturn your carriage.'

'I have not done so yet, so do not see why I should do so on this journey.' He turned and gave her a gentle push towards the door. 'Goodnight, little one, sleep well. I will see you again in four weeks.'

Eleanor smiled at him, raised her hand in a farewell gesture, then retired to her room to spend her first night as a married woman, alone. She tossed sleeplessly, in her large empty bed, and Leo paced in frustration, back and forth in the study, until the early hours of the morning. She heard him come up and walk quietly to his room at dawn. His carriage was summoned and he left, neither of them having slept.

After his departure, Eleanor finally fell asleep and lay, log-like, until she was awoken with her hot chocolate, at eight o'clock. As her maid bustled about she sipped her drink, letting the rich, smooth drink soothe her ragged nerves.

'Can you find me that very old habit, Mary? You know the one you said was fit only for the bonfire.'

'Whatever next!' Mary exclaimed, but found the required garment without further protest. She had worked for her young mistress for more than five years and recognized the sound of trouble when she heard it. If her ladyship was up to mischief now his lordship was away it was no longer her place to interfere.

Eleanor washed and dressed in her disreputable habit sent Mary on a search for some boy's boots. 'I need some stout boots, Mary, the sort Tom, the stable boy, wears. Do you think you could find me some? I do not wish you to take them off anybody's feet but purchase them. You know my size well enough.'

'Yes, my lady,' Mary answered politely. 'I will go and look for those boots right away.'

Eleanor watched her go, sad that their closeness appeared to be over. She recognized that, as a married woman, and a lady, even if it was only a courtesy title, the informal relationship she had had with her maid had to stop. She hoped she would not now be expected to adopt a style of address that her Aunt Prudence had used for her personal maid and call Mary by her second name, Thompson.

She wondered why things couldn't stay the same. It did not seem fair that everything must change because she had a ring on her finger. She was still exactly the same person she had been yesterday morning, and it was not only her relationship with Mary that she was thinking of.

After a solitary breakfast of toast and honey, washed down with weak tea she was ready to tackle her Grand Plan. But first she needed to speak to Sam; he was an integral part of her scheme and she was delighted her husband had, so thoughtfully, left him behind. She sent one of the footmen in search of her unsuspecting assistant and waited impatiently for his appearance in the small salon.

Sam arrived at the same time as Mary and the boots. 'Thank you, Mary, these are excellent. I will not require you until three o'clock.'

'Very well, my lady.' Mary bobbed a curtsy

and turned to leave.

'Oh Mary, could you continue to supervise the sewing for me? I will be too busy elsewhere from now on.'

'Yes, of course. Will that be all, my lady?'

Sam had been standing, watching this exchange with interest. Lord Upminster had left him behind for the sole purpose of keeping an eye on his wife, and to try and prevent her from getting into further scrapes.

'Sam, thank you for coming so promptly,' Eleanor began. 'I need your help with a plan I have.' She smiled at him sunnily, filling his heart with foreboding. 'His lordship, I am sure, told you he had given me *carte blanche* where alterations and improvements were concerned; is that correct?'

Sam nodded miserably, sensing, like Mary, that trouble was coming his way. 'Yes, my lady, I know that.'

'Good. I intend to renovate and renew the farm cottages in the dip, just before the lane reaches the village.' She raised her head from lacing up her sturdy, brown boots. 'Is it not a brilliant scheme, Sam?'

Sam was at a loss, a rare occurrence for him. 'I am not sure Lord Upminster intended you to' — he hesitated, not wishing to use the word interfere — 'to become involved with alterations outside the Hall itself, my lady.'

'Oh fiddlesticks to that! He said I could alter and improve whatever I wished, and I wish to improve those cottages and I need your help to do so.' She gave him a charming, if conspiratorial, smile. 'Anyway we should have finished long before Lord Upminster returns, and what is done cannot be undone, can it?'

He could not resist her smile. He knew his master would be hopping mad but as he had been instructed to help in any way he could he wasn't breaking any promises.

'I have asked for the pony cart to be brought round; I would like you to come with me to inspect what needs doing. I can see they are in a sad state of repair but what actually has to be done, I will leave up to you to decide.' Her strangely shod feet clumped through the house and almost startled Brown as he waited to open the front door for them.

The short drive to the cottages was accomplished in less than twenty minutes.

'Do the cottagers know that their houses are to be improved, my lady?' Sam enquired, as Eleanor halted the cart, expertly, outside the dilapidated homes.

'No, but I am sure they will be delighted; anyone would be if their homes were to be made sound and waterproof.'

'I hope that you are right, my lady; some

folks don't appreciate change,' Sam told her, hoping his prediction might prove correct. If the occupants refused to co-operate then nothing could be done and his worries would be over.

Eleanor jumped nimbly from the cart and headed for the cottage in the middle of the row. She knew that the key family resided there, for she had sometimes taken baskets of goods to them at Aunt Prudence's request. Sam knocked at the door loudly, surprised his fist had not pushed it from its hinges.

The door was opened, with difficulty, by a sharp-eyed woman, with several small children hanging from her, clean, but well-worn skirts.

'Good morning, Mrs Smith. Is Mr Smith at home? I would like to speak to him, if that is possible,' Eleanor asked courteously.

Mrs Smith dropped a nominal curtsy and stepped aside. 'You'd better come in then, my lady,' she said, but didn't seem especially pleased by the prospect.

Eleanor followed her into the dark interior; she had to duck her head to avoid hitting it on the door frame. Sam followed her in, unwilling to let her out of his sight. Smith, a man of medium height and build, greeted them politely, but with little more enthusiasm than his wife.

''Mornin', my lady. What can I do for you?' His tone was correct, but not servile.

Mrs Smith remembered her manners. 'Won't you be seated, my lady? Can I get you anything?'

'No, thank you, Mrs Smith,' Eleanor replied. Smith had remained standing, as had Sam.

'Please do sit down, Mr Smith, I wish to talk to you about something I hope you will be happy about.'

The taciturn man sat on a stool by the fire and waited patiently for her to enlighten him. 'I would like, with your permission of course, to repair and improve this row of cottages.'

Mr Smith gaped at her. 'Repair? Our permission? I should say you have it, my lady. I've been on at the agent, Jed Timpson, but he has said that there ain't no funds for repairs.'

Eleanor looked at Sam triumphantly. 'So you will be happy for the cottages to be repaired, Mr Smith?'

'I'll say I would, and so would all the rest.'

'I realize November is not an ideal time to start repairs, but I wanted you all to be snug for Christmas.' She stood up and indicated Sam. 'Sam Roberts, Lord Upminster's man, will talk to you and make a note of everything that needs doing. I wish to install water, as

125

well, in every kitchen, if that is possible.'

Smith turned to his wife in amazement. 'You hear that, Dolly, water in here! Who'd have thought it!'

Eleanor smiled; delighted her news had been well received. 'I thought that if we started the end cottage first, maybe the Bishops could move in with someone else until the work is finished. What do you think, Mr Smith?'

He beamed at her; she might be a snippet of a thing, and only married for five minutes to his lordship, but she was a true lady. 'Nora and Jim, and the nippers, can move in with Fred and his missis the other side; they have no babes, so have more room.'

'Excellent,' Eleanor said, drawing on her gloves. 'I will leave you to sort out the details with Mr Roberts, good morning.'

This time the entire family either bowed, or dropped a curtsy, every face wreathed in delighted smiles. On the journey back to Monk's Hall, Eleanor was determined to see the agent and persuade him to co-operate in her scheme as well.

The fact that Leo would be livid at her interference in his domain was something she refused to think about. Whatever his reaction, and she expected it to be bad, he could not undo any work that had been done. Knowing the five families would spend a warm and comfortable Christmas because of her actions would more than compensate for anything her formidable husband might say or do.

And anyway, she thought, I don't have to worry about his return for another four weeks, and maybe he will have missed me so much that he will overlook my behaviour completely. Even if she didn't really believe this, it did give her a small degree of comfort.

Eleanor went in search of Jed Timpson, and her grand scheme to use her new position to better the lot of those less fortunate, swung into action.

12

The finishing touches were being applied to the last cottage on the Tuesday of the fourth week of Leo's absence. Eleanor had worked her magic and managed to involve Jed Timpson, the agent, as well as most of the staff from Monk's Hall. Mrs Basingstoke had been persuaded to part with sheets, blankets and table covers that were too worn to be repaired. Then Eleanor's seamstresses busily turned these remnants into curtains, bed covering and other things, for the cottages.

Brown had been prevailed upon to send his footman up into the attics to unearth pieces of broken and unwanted furniture. Craftsmen from the village were employed to repair and restore these items and then they were also given to the cottagers.

Eleanor had helped in whatever way she could by fetching and carrying in the pony cart as required. At no time did the tenants, and villagers she worked with, take advantage of her kindness. It did not need Sam's presence to ensure that she was treated with the utmost respect.

Up to her boot tops in mud, she stepped

back to admire the completed homes. 'I am so pleased we have finished before the rain sets in, Sam. Everybody has worked so hard; I think we should hold a celebration to mark the occasion.'

Sam was dubious; cottages were one thing, but a party for the staff was even more unsuitable for Lady Upminster to be involved with.

'Do not frown so, Sam. I was not thinking of a large event. We could clear the barn that the craftsmen have been working in and then put some hay bales in for seats. Then all we need is some music, food and drink.'

'We'd best keep it short, my lady, a couple of hours would do.'

Having secured a partial victory, Eleanor was satisfied and rushed off to discuss her plans with Mrs Smith, who she knew, would organize everything for her.

The celebration was arranged for the following afternoon and ale and lemonade were to be provided by the Hall. Mrs Smith had arranged that the food would be supplied by the tenants themselves. Two fiddlers, and a man on a penny whistle, had volunteered to supply the music. Brown and the house-keeper had agreed that any member of staff who had previously given up their own time to help in the project could have the two hours off to attend.

Eleanor was pleased with what she had achieved. She felt that for the first time she had done something worthwhile; she was justifiably proud of the work and her part in it. It was unfortunate that Lord Upminster did not share her view.

He returned at two o'clock on the Wednesday and found his home deserted. However, the sound of merriment could quite clearly be heard coming from one of the old barns a half-mile from the Hall. As he was striding purposefully in the direction of the noise, he met Jed Timpson, who greeted him happily, glad that his lordship had returned in time for the celebration.

'Good afternoon, my lord, you have arrived in time to see the home-warming party. The cottages look splendid, I'm sure you will agree.'

'Which cottages would these be, exactly?' Lord Upminster said silkily, only his narrowed eyes giving warning of his mood.

'The cottages by the . . . ' Jed's voice trailed away as he realized, to his horror, that his employer knew nothing about the renovations.

'Go on man,' Leo said, sharply. 'I am waiting, what cottages?'

'You didn't know. Oh dear,' Jed muttered,

seeing his career as an agent about to be terminated. 'I never would have, if I had known, my lord,' he babbled, Leo's glare quite unnerving him.

'Stop rambling, Timpson. Tell me what's been happening in my absence, now, if you please.' The authority in his voice sobered Jed who hastily explained what Lady Upminster had been up to.

'And now they are having a little party to celebrate, my lord,' he finished.

Leo had listened in disbelief to his normally sensible agent tell him how the whole household had been inveigled by his wife in an escapade that they must all have known was not sanctioned by him. Seething with suppressed anger he strode off to the barn to confront his devious, and disappointing, wife.

Eleanor, knowing it would be very improper, had wisely refrained from joining in the celebration. She watched the twirling figures happily from the side, enjoying their uninhibited pleasure. It was there that her husband found her.

However angry he was with his wife he would not let his disapproval spoil the party for his people. They had little enough to celebrate in the hard life they led. He walked over, with a smile of apparent approval, that didn't reach his eyes, to join Eleanor.

'Lady Upminster, I hate to ask you to leave such a jolly occasion, but I have several rather important things to tell you, and require you to accompany me back to the Hall.' His tone was calm, even friendly, but she recognized instantly that he was enraged.

She smiled brightly and stepped away from him. 'Good afternoon, my lord, we did not expect you back so soon. Did you have a successful trip?'

'We can discuss that, in my study, my dear,' he said, through gritted teeth. He gripped her arm firmly ensuring she could not escape. 'We will go in now, if you please.'

Eleanor replied quietly so only he could hear. 'I am not going in, Leo, and unless you intend to drag me behind you I suggest that you let go my arm and go away. Your scowl will spoil the party.'

Slowly he released her arm, then, his face rigid, he said equally quietly, 'I will be waiting for you when you do return, Eleanor, be very sure of that.' He walked away, smiling a greeting here and there, as though he was as happy as they were about the party.

Mary was appalled by Eleanor's behaviour and forgot to address her formally. 'Miss Ellie, you should not have said that. You should have gone with him.'

'But he was so angry, Mary; I thought if I went later he would have had time to calm down.'

When she saw the look on Mary's face she began to realize that she might have made a grave error of judgement. 'He will be even angrier now. How could I have been so stupid?'

For a minute or two she stood trying to decide what to do. She came to a decision; if Mary was right, and she feared she was, the longer she left it the worse the reckoning would be. 'I am going in now.' Her maid started to follow her. 'No, stay here, enjoy the party; I will go back on my own.'

'That you won't, my lady,' Mary told her firmly. 'Sam Roberts can walk back with you, if you don't need me.'

Sam was found and walked silently across the field beside her. 'His lordship often sounds harsher than he intends, my lady, and I'm sure he would never really hurt you, however angry he is,' he said, hoping his words would remove the look of apprehension that was playing across Eleanor's face.

'Thank you, Sam, I am sure you are right. It is my own fault because I knew he would be angry; I have just made it worse by refusing to accompany him when he asked me.'

They completed the journey in silence. Some of the words Sam had spoken to allay her fears kept rattling around her skull. He had said that Leo would not really hurt her — what had he meant? She had a nasty, sinking feeling that whatever Leo had promised previously, she was in for a very unpleasant time indeed.

Sam left her at the door to face her fate alone. She decided she couldn't go straight to the study in her faded dress and boy's boots; she would feel a little less vulnerable wearing something more sophisticated. Not having the assistance of her maid it took Eleanor much longer than she would have wished, to wash, change and tidy her hair. She felt sure that Leo already knew she was back because Brown, ever vigilant, had seen her going upstairs.

Finally satisfied that Leo would find no fault with her appearance she prepared to go down. She was dreading the forthcoming encounter but the pride she felt in her accomplishment was giving her courage. She would not let her fearsome husband have it all his own way.

The crash of the door suddenly slamming open made her cry out in shock. Leo erupted into the room and banged the door shut behind him. Eleanor stared dumbly at the stranger standing, legs apart, glaring at her, his eyes like flint.

Then, strangely, her fear vanished and indignation at Leo's rude arrival took over. She, in her turn, raked him from the top of his dark head to the toes of his polished boots, with studied disdain. 'I do not believe I gave you leave to enter my bedchamber, my lord,' she stated coldly.

'I am your husband; I do not need your permission to enter any room in this house,' he snarled, his fury fanned by her apparent disregard. 'If you had come, as you were told, to the study, there would have been no call for me to be here.'

Eleanor raised her eyebrows, and pursed her lips but did not reply. She knew she was in the right but felt it to be unwise to say so. 'Now you are here, my lord,' she deliberately emphasized the formal appellation, 'perhaps we should sit down.' Eleanor gestured to the two chairs placed on either side of the window. Without waiting for his agreement she moved to the chair on the left and sat down, taking the time it gave her, to arrange her skirts and gather her wits.

Leo remained where he was. 'I am deeply disappointed in you, Eleanor. I knew you were unconventional, and given to rash impulses, but never did I think that you would sink to such depths. You have, by your appalling behaviour, disgraced yourself and me.' He paused, wishing to choose his next words carefully, wanting his wife to understand the enormity of her actions.

Eleanor had heard enough. 'I will apologize for going ahead with the renovations without your explicit consent; I will also sincerely apologize for my incivility earlier. However, I will not apologize for what I did; I am proud of what has been accomplished and if society condemns me for doing good, then so be it.' Her voice throughout her speech had remained composed and polite. For the first time she had been able to put forward her point of view, without fear, even in the face of Leo's formidable temper.

The tightness around Leo's jaw relaxed somewhat and he strolled over and sat down on the chair next to her. 'I would appear to have been thoroughly routed, Eleanor, my dear,' he said after a few moments. 'In the face of your unanswerable logic I believe that it is now my turn to apologize.' A slight smile accompanied his words but his face was still far from friendly. Eleanor breathed an audible sigh of relief, believing her ordeal was over. 'However,' he continued, 'I am still extremely displeased with you, Eleanor.' He faced her with a stern expression. 'I believe I explained to you your position in this marriage. Your decisions are strictly limited to the household, and nowhere else. To involve Sam and Jed in your scheme was not well done; it put them in an impossible position. You should have realized that they risked dismissal for helping you.'

Eleanor was horrified; this had not occurred to her. 'But you will not do so, will you? Please, Leo, I do not care how you punish me but you cannot send Sam and Jed away, it was my fault.'

It was Leo's turn to sigh heavily. 'You are impossible, Ellie. You do the most appalling things and then somehow manage to disarm me totally.' He smiled and this time it was genuine. 'If I agree to say no more on the subject, will you promise me never to go behind my back again?'

She returned his smile, scarcely believing that she was to come out of this unscathed. 'I promise, Leo. I knew you would be cross, but never considered how others might be affected by my action; that was truly wrong of me. Will you forgive me? I have learned my lesson.'

Leo could not resist her appeal. 'Of course I do, ninny; it is impossible to stay angry with you for long.' He stood up, pulling her to her feet as well, a quite different kind of darkness in his eyes. As he gathered her into his embrace he murmured softly into her ears 'Well, little bird, have you missed me?'

She tilted her head back to gaze into his eyes. 'Oh yes, I have.' A gurgle of laughter escaped unbidden, 'But I am glad that you stayed away long enough for us to complete the cottages.'

He tightened his clasp and crushed her against him, his mouth closing over hers in a hot, demanding kiss. Eleanor's knees buckled under his onslaught and he caught her up in his arms and, without hesitation, carried her across the room to deposit her softly in the centre of her bed.

She stared helplessly at him as he shrugged out of his jacket and removed his cravat. If she wanted this to stop, now was the time to speak; when he joined her on the bed it would be too late. Was she ready? Could she bear to share her body with a man who didn't love her?

Leo had watched the expressions of doubt flicker across her face and somehow he found the strength to resist. Carefully he backed away from the bed until he had put a safe distance between them. 'I am sorry, sweetheart, I am finding this so difficult, but you are still not quite sure about sharing your bed, are you?'

Eleanor had not realized her face was so easily read. She sat up and put her feet back on the floor. 'If you wish to' — she hesitated, not sure how to phrase what she wished to say — 'if you wish to make love to me I will not stop you . . . but if you are giving me a choice then yes, I would prefer to wait. I know four weeks have passed, but we were apart the entire time, and are still no better acquainted.'

He was almost tempted to accept the offer, but as a gentleman he knew he could never force the issue. 'No, love, I will wait until you come to me; that way I can be sure of your feelings.' He picked up his mangled neckcloth and coat and turned to leave. 'I had better speak to Jed and Sam; they must be feeling very vulnerable at the moment.'

'I will be down soon, Leo. I want to hear everything that happened in London.'

As she watched her husband leave the room Eleanor was happy. For all his harsh words, and fiery temper, she had come to realize that he was a kind and sensitive man. She had fallen in love with him, in spite of his faults, and knew that she would always love him, however he behaved, and whatever he did. It would just make things so much easier if he could return her love, even a little.

13

'But Rufus will not lead; John tried it before.' Eleanor would not give up on her determination to take the horse with them to Rothmere, even if she couldn't ride him when she got there.

'If you think I am going to ride him all the way there, in the middle of December, you have sadly mistaken the matter, my dear girl.'

How she hated it when he adopted that patronizing manner. 'If he does not come, neither shall I.'

Leo laughed at her. 'You are a ninny. You know you would hate to stay here on your own, and anyway I would not allow it. Therefore I am afraid it will be Rufus who stays. If I leave Hero to keep him company, will that suffice?'

She almost stamped her foot. 'No, it will not, but as I have no choice in the matter it will be what happens, no doubt.' She stormed out of the drawing-room, leaving Leo chuckling, hatefully, behind her.

Eleanor ran upstairs to change out of her pale-gold, long-sleeved, dimity day dress into her old riding habit. Mary hung up her clothes without comment; she knew what the disagreement was about. Indeed the whole house knew, as the heated discussions had been taking place, loudly, for the last two days.

On the way to the stable Eleanor had a brainwave. Rufus wouldn't be led but he would follow her of his own accord. 'John,' she called excitedly, as she arrived in the yard, 'can you get the travelling carriage for me?'

John appeared, his face perplexed. 'I'm sorry, my lady, I had not been told you were going out today. I will get the horses put to at once.'

'We are not going out; I wish to try something before we leave tomorrow.' She laughed, unwilling to explain her plan in case he objected and sent for Leo.

John called Tommy, the stable boy, and another groom and in no time the carriage was ready, the four matching greys chomping eagerly at the bit. Eleanor felt it would be safe to reveal her plan now; it was too late for Leo to interfere, even if he was sent for.

'I am going to let Rufus out and see if he will follow the carriage when I am in it. If he does he will be able to come with us tomorrow and you can ride Hero and keep an eye on him.'

What John thought of her harebrained

scheme he was too polite to say. 'Right you are, my lady. Where do you want us to drive?'

'Around the park at first, and if it works, we can go to the village and back,' she answered briskly, sounding far more confident than she felt.

Leo could not understand her reluctance to be apart from the horse. He had pointed out, quite reasonably, that she had left Rufus behind for a year when she went to India and they had both survived the experience. She was beginning to wonder if she was only insisting on his coming because her husband had said he could not. Well, it was too late to worry about that; she was going to see if her idea worked before agreeing to leave him behind.

Rufus was rather surprised to be led out and then released to stand, loose, beside the carriage. Eleanor scrambled up quickly and Tommy shut the carriage door and folded the steps away. She lowered the window and, hanging out, called her horse. Rufus immediately pricked his ears and trotted forward to try and push his huge head through the window.

'Go away, you stupid animal,' she said, laughing, and stroked his nose. 'Right, John, pull away, slowly.'

The carriage rolled forward and the

chestnut stallion kept pace; as long as he could follow his mistress he would do so happily. The odd group had trotted and cantered around the park for half an hour when Eleanor decided they could risk a drive to the village. The lanes were too narrow to allow the horse to travel beside the window and she wanted to see if he would follow, safely, behind the carriage.

She had forgotten their exit ran past the study window where Leo was working. They had travelled only a short distance when a roared command to stop was clearly heard by all of them. The carriage instantly shuddered to a standstill, the horses tossing their heads at the delay. Eleanor was tempted to shrink into the corner but bravely decided to meet Leo head on.

She moved across and leant out of the window to see her husband approaching rapidly. He did not look overly impressed by her bright idea. Rufus, recognizing a friend, welcomed him with an affectionate nudge that, catching Leo unprepared, sent him sprawling in the dirt.

She jumped out, not waiting for the steps, and rushed over to help him up. 'Leo, oh dear, I should have warned you he sometimes does that. Rufus, go away, you have caused enough trouble already,' she told the horse who was curious to discover why his friend was on the ground.

Leo rolled over, spitting out a mouthful of gravel and dirt as he did so. 'In God's name, Ellie, what are you doing? Why is this stupid animal running about loose?' Eleanor opened her mouth to explain but he stopped her. 'No, I do not want to hear. It is bound to be something completely idiotic that I end up agreeing to support.' He sprang to his feet and, without saying anything else, picked her up and tossed her, unceremoniously, back into the carriage. Then he jumped in after her and slammed the door. He poked his head out of the window and spoke to John, sitting impassively on the box. 'Carry on doing, whatever it is you are doing, John.' As the carriage resumed its journey he smiled down at his dumbfounded wife. 'I shall sit here, my angel, as an interested spectator and no doubt, eventually, all will be revealed and I will discover what pea-brained scheme you are involved with this time.'

Eleanor did not know whether to applaud his speech or box his ears. 'I should have thought,' she told him haughtily, 'that even to a simpleton like you, my lord, it would have been obvious.'

Her long-suffering husband was having difficulty keeping a straight face but schooled his features into a look of such imbecility that Eleanor lost her patience completely. Launching herself from the seat she attempted to give her husband a well-deserved box on the ears.

Instead she found herself, quite inexplicably, face down, across his knees. Before she could protest, or wriggle free, he delivered a resounding slap on her posterior. Then he flipped her upright again, openly grinning, and held her at arm's length.

'Little termagant! I am almost twice your size, sweetheart; did you honestly think your attack would be successful?'

'You are a bully, Lord Upminster, and you have just broken your word. You promised you would never raise a hand to me,' she said indignantly, not sure whether to laugh or cry.

'It serves you right,' he replied unsympathetically. 'I have just swallowed a shovelful of gravel because of you; one slap in return seems fair.' He shoved her, none too gently, back on to the seat opposite, before continuing; 'Now sit still and tell me what the hell you are up to.'

Eleanor scowled darkly, still undecided whether she was speaking to him or not. Rufus then answered Leo's question for him by sticking his nose in the window and whickering a greeting, then dropping back to trot beside the carriage.

Leo stared at the window at the horse, then back at Ellie. 'You are either a genius or a madwoman, Lady Upminster. Do you intend that daft horse to follow us, like a puppy, all the way to Rothmere, tomorrow?'

She nodded, not really certain whether he was praising her plan, or ridiculing it. 'He has always followed me when I have been on foot so I thought he would probably continue to do it if I was in the carriage.'

'It is a wonderful plan, my darling, but will he still follow if the carriage window is closed?' At her blank expression he continued, 'I do not intend to travel for hours, in the depths of winter, with my carriage window wide open.'

Eleanor shook her head. 'I had not thought of that.'

'Well, we had better see if he does.' Leo pulled up the window and fastened it firmly. They sat opposite each other, arms folded, listening for the sound of hoofbeats outside.

The flap opened in the roof and John called down from the box, 'The horse is still following behind, my lady, good as gold.'

'Thank you, John; we can turn back now we know my plan works.'

'You never cease to amaze me, Eleanor,' Leo told her. 'I suppose this means that we are to arrive at Rothmere tomorrow with a loose horse trotting along behind, like something out of a damn circus parade.'

Eleanor chuckled. 'We do not have to take Rufus, Leo, if it will embarrass you.'

'Not take him? After all this fuss? No, Rufus comes too.' He smiled, as a thought occurred to him. 'In fact, I insist he comes. It will be interesting to see the duke's reaction.'

★ ★ ★

The strange cavalcade set off before dawn the next day; the coachman on his box, with Sam beside him, and John, riding Hero, and with Rufus running loose. Inside, Mary was next to Eleanor and Leo occupied the seat opposite. The trunks, and other necessities, had left the previous day so that their clothes could be unpacked and waiting for them on their arrival.

They made excellent time and after two brief stops for refreshments, and to rest the horses, they were within one hour of Leo's birthplace. 'From this point on, the land belongs to Rothmere,' Leo informed his wife. 'We should arrive in about an hour.'

Eleanor had known the estate was huge, but to be able to travel for an hour, in a straight line, and still be on Rothmere land, made her realize just how extensive it was. 'How many guests will there be, do you think, Leo?' she asked, a few moments later. As they drew nearer the thought of meeting dozens of Leo's aristocratic relatives was beginning to unnerve her.

'I have no idea, Eleanor, does it matter to you? You are not worried about meeting them, are you?'

'Not really; I was just curious. You have told me so little about your family; I ought to know who is married to whom, at the very least.'

Leo straightened, realizing she was right. 'Then I will start with Gareth and Sophia, shall I, and work outwards?' Eleanor nodded eager to learn about his relations. He continued, 'Gareth and Sophia have three boys; Tristan, the eldest who is ten, Gareth who is eight and little Leo, who is, I think, now about four.'

The rest of the journey was filled pleasantly with Leo reciting the names, ranks and marital status of all the various cousins, aunts, uncles and in-laws who were likely to be staying for the festivities. When he had completed his catalogue Eleanor looked at him with awe.

'Do you realize that without children that will be over thirty? If everyone brings five servants, as we have, that will be more than one hundred extra mouths to feed and house.' She could hardly take it in. 'Rothmere must be huge to accommodate so many people.'

'It is huge. In fact, Ellie, it is a monstrosity. It is an ancient pile that should be pulled down immediately and rebuilt on a more manageable scale.' Eleanor looked shocked at his vehement criticism, especially as it was in front of Mary. 'I loathe the place and only agreed to visit for your sake. Gareth persuaded me that it was my duty to introduce you to everyone, and Sophia told me that if I was not intending to take you to London for a season, that the least I could do was bring you to Rothmere, so you can wear your new clothes.'

'Thank you, Leo, but I would not have minded if we had stayed at home, although I am happy to be here.' Eleanor reached across and pressed his arm to reinforce her thanks.

'I hope you enjoy it. But I feel it only fair to warn you, Ellie, that I have not set foot in this place since I left some fifteen years ago.'

'Never come here? Surely not? You have seen Gareth and Sophia and the children?'

'They come to London for the season most years and I stayed with them when I was on leave.' He glanced out of the window sensing they were almost there. It was now fully dark and the interior of the carriage was becoming unpleasantly stuffy, and cold. Eleanor could sense the tension in her husband as the carriage rolled to a stop and there was the sound of voices, and lanterns appeared outside the window.

Impulsively she joined Leo and placed her fingers around his clenched fist. For a moment he was unresponsive then, slowly, his fingers uncurled and threaded through hers. He closed his fist again, her small hand engulfed in his.

He twisted around and lowered his head to whisper, for her benefit alone, 'You will be the most beautiful woman at Rothmere, my darling, and I am the luckiest man alive.'

On their arrival, the steps had been lowered by an immaculate footman and the carriage door swung open. Leo ducked his head and stepped out, temporarily releasing his hold on Eleanor's hand. On the bottom step, he swung round, reached in and clasped her around the waist, then lifted her out, in a flurry of petticoats, to stand right beside him, her hand once more entwined with his.

They both remembered, at the same time, about the horse. 'Rufus!' Hearing his name the stallion snatched his head from John's hold and barged round to greet his owners.

The two unlucky footmen, who were standing politely to one side, waiting to guide the visitors in, did not stand a chance. Half a ton of excited stallion hit them in the back and the next thing they knew they were, like Leo the previous day, face down in the gravel. Rufus, like all of his kind, preferred not to step on humans, so walked over them, adding to their terror.

Leo calmly took hold of his halter with his free hand and, shoulders shaking with suppressed mirth, led both Rufus, and his wife, round to the stable block.

14

The manner of Lord and Lady Upminster's arrival would not have gone unnoticed. Word had been relayed to the duke, ensconced in his palatial apartments in the East Wing and he was not amused. By the time Rufus had been safely installed in a loose box, Eleanor's nervousness had flown. She was more concerned about removing all signs of the stable yard from her smart, dark-gold pelisse and straightening her pretty poke bonnet.

Mary finished her ministrations at last. 'There, my lady, you look smart as paint. No one would know you had been visiting the stable.' Mary's tone suggested Eleanor should have known better. Satisfied all was as it should be, Eleanor slipped her hand through Leo's waiting arm.

'I am ready now; Gareth and Sophia must be wondering what has become of us.'

Leo grinned. 'No doubt they have already been informed of the spectacle we made on our arrival. Now, let us go in.' He glared in mock severity at his wife. 'And please, my love, do not say anything outrageous, or laugh immoderately, this is a house where humour is not allowed.'

'You are an idiot, Leo Upminster,' she giggled, 'and far worse than I.'

Leo led Eleanor round to the grand front entrance where the butler and housekeeper were keeping watch for them.

'Good evening, my lord, my lady, welcome home.' Melville gave a low, reverential bow. The housekeeper curtsied and they were ushered into the enormous entrance hall. The icy blast that accompanied them reminded Eleanor of Leo's disparaging comments on the lack of comfort at Rothmere. They were taken upstairs immediately and were informed that dinner would be served in forty-five minutes.

Eleanor's room was huge and gloomy, furnished with oldfashioned, heavy dark wood. An intimidating, brocade hung, four-poster bed dominated the far wall. Although there was a large fire burning merrily in the grate, the room was freezing. She could see the window curtains moving in the draught.

Leo had followed her in. 'I warned you that the rooms are uncomfortable and cold, my dear.' He pointed to a door in the panelling. 'I am through there; the door is not locked.' Eleanor felt herself flushing as he reminded

153

her of the promise to go to him when she was ready.

She swallowed quickly, and then turned away shyly.

'I will leave you to dress, Ellie. I will come for you in forty minutes. Rothmere does not employ a gong; the place is so big no one would hear it.' He strode to the communicating door and then paused. 'Wear the rose crepe tonight, Eleanor.' Having issued his order he vanished through the door.

Eleanor was ready before the stated time and she paced the room, hoping activity would keep her warm. Even with the addition of a beautiful cashmere shawl, her evening dress was too flimsy for a room as cold as hers; she prayed the reception rooms downstairs would be warmer.

A light tap on the door heralded Leo's arrival. He stepped through, immaculate in black. 'You look breathtaking, my love.' His eyes reflected his frank appreciation. 'Are you ready? Good, then we will go down. Remember never to venture out of your room alone; you might get lost and starve to death before anyone finds you.'

His joke made her laugh and she was still smiling, looking lovely, when they arrived at the main salon. The butler announced them and the gaze of all the occupants focused in their direction. Leo proudly led his new wife to meet her relatives. Eleanor curtsied and smiled and offered her hand to so many elegant people that she feared she would never be able to distinguish one cousin, aunt, or uncle from another. The one person she really wanted to meet was conspicuous by his absence: the Duke of Rothmere would not be joining them for dinner as he was indisposed.

Leo turned to Gareth in disgust. 'He is never indisposed. He has never had a day's illness in his life; he is without doubt one of the healthiest seventy-year-olds in the land.'

'The duke is playing his usual games, Leo. Do not cut up about it. You can go and see him tomorrow; it will be better to become reacquainted in privacy, surely?'

Eleanor agreed with her brother-in-law. 'I am relieved. I would much prefer to meet his grace, for the first time, in his own apartments.'

Leo relaxed and captured Ellie's hand. 'I hope you are not expecting to charm him, darling; he has a heart of stone.'

Dinner was announced before Eleanor could answer. Gareth headed the line with Sophia, dressed in a stunning gown made from the gold, Indian-figured silk she had been given. Eleanor, to her surprise, found that she and Leo were halfway down the procession and she commented on this, in a whisper, to her husband.

'I am a lowly second son and do not hold the title in my own right, Ellie.' He frowned, obviously remembering a past annoyance. 'Although there is a title, and property, which I could have had if the duke had wished to give it to me.'

'You have no need of a title of your own, Leo, or another property. We have more than we need.'

'But any children that we have will be commoners.'

'I am a commoner and none the worse for it. I do not believe any children we might have will suffer either.' She wished to reassure Leo that she was more than happy with what they had. She failed to notice the small smile of satisfaction on his face because she had accepted, as fact, that at some point they would be having children.

Even with thirty seated around the table each was marooned in an individual sea of cutlery and crystal. Eleanor was grateful her place was beside Leo and they were able to converse quietly throughout the meal. He kept her entertained with scurrilous anecdotes about the various members of his family scattered around the room. He drew her attention to a dandy, in a violently striped waistcoat, and shirt points so high he could hardly turn his head.

'Avoid that macaroni; he is a distant cousin of mine, infamous for his behaviour. Scandal follows him like a bad smell.'

'What is his name? I have never met a black sheep. He looks ridiculous; I cannot believe anyone with sense would take him seriously.'

'Sir Bertram Jenkins. I am not funning, Ellie, he is dangerous; avoid him.'

Their conversation ended as the marchioness rose regally at the end of the elaborate dinner and led the ladies through to the grand salon. Eleanor was delighted when Leo appeared with the other gentlemen shortly afterwards for she had been finding the constant questioning from the ladies of rank quite exhausting. He threaded his way through the love seats and *chaise-longue* to drop, nonchalantly, beside her, much to the astonishment of an elderly, be-turbaned dowager.

'Good heavens, girl, who is this man?' Leo's great-aunt Agatha had failed to recognize him.

'I am your great-nephew, Leo Upminster, your grace, and I have come to talk to my wife. I hope you have no objection?'

'Actually, I have.' Her tone was garrulous. 'I would have thought there was enough

157

conversation between you in the bedroom.' She stood up and nodded at a rapidly reddening Eleanor. 'I would talk some more with you, young lady. You speak more sense than anyone else I have met here.' Leo, who had leapt to his feet, bowed again, and watched his great-aunt disappear towards a sea of similar turbans.

'Thank goodness you came, Leo. It was only a matter of time before I said something to disgrace myself.'

Leo was sympathetic. 'Poor love; elderly relatives are a sore trial to the young.' He grinned down at her as he rejoined her on the seat. 'But console yourself, my dear; one day you will be an elderly interfering relative yourself.'

Eleanor stifled her giggles in the corner of her shawl, remembering Leo's semi-jocular instruction not to laugh out loud. 'Ellie, what on earth are you doing? You look as though you are blowing your nose on that.'

'Sorry,' she spluttered, 'but you said that I was not allowed to laugh. I do not recall that wiping my nose on my wrap was forbidden.' She peeked at him, green eyes brimming with mischief, from behind her shawl.

'Baggage! Do you want to wait for tea, or shall we escape now?'

'I would love to go but will it seem uncivil?'

'No, they will think we are newlywed and going upstairs to celebrate the fact.' He had taken Eleanor's hands and raised her to her feet as he spoke so she had no option but to leave with him, her face, yet again a becoming shade of pink. A footman lit them to their rooms and on arrival opened Eleanor's door with a flourish. He waited for her to walk through and was astounded when Lord Upminster followed her and quietly closed the door in his face.

'Leo, you should not have come in here.'

'Why not? I am your husband and you are my wife, what could be more natural?'

'A more modest gentlemen would have entered this room by the connecting door, not walked brazenly in with his wife,' she scolded.

In answer, he took her gently in his arms and feathered kisses across her face, sending delicious tingles up and down her spine. Of her own volition she pressed closer, loving the feel of his hardness against her soft curves. To her consternation he immediately broke the embrace, unhooked her hands from behind his head, and moved away.

'No, Ellie, my love; my resolve is strong, but being so near to you is testing me to breaking.' His mouth curved in a dark, warm smile. 'You must not keep me waiting too long, darling; this is driving me insane.' He left her there, wanting to follow him, but with legs that remained rooted to the floor.

Mary appeared from the dressing-room. 'I'm sorry, my lady, I didn't realize you had come up. I hope I haven't kept you waiting long?'

'Not at all; I want to be up early tomorrow to explore, so please lay out my green worsted walking dress, with the matching pelisse and bonnet, and also my heavy boots. You did pack them, I hope?'

'Yes, my Lady, I did. But I'm not sure you should wear such things here.'

'Nonsense, they are warm and weather-proof and no one will see them beneath my skirt anyway.'

When Eleanor was alone she crept across the darkened room, her candlestick in her hand, to place her ear against the dividing wall. She didn't know what noises she expected to hear but the sound of marching feet was certainly not one of them. She slipped, like a wraith in her long, white nightgown, back to the enormous four-poster bed. Ignoring the steps, thoughtfully provided, she scrambled on to the soft feather mattress. The sheets were still warm from the hot bricks Mary had put in earlier. With the curtains drawn round it was almost cosy and she fell asleep immediately.

* * *

Next morning dawned crisp and cold, the grass silvered with frost and the lake frozen hard. Eleanor ignored her chocolate drink in her eagerness to dress and go out to confirm, or deny, Leo's scathing description of Rothmere.

'Do hurry, Mary. I want to breakfast before everyone else is down and then go out for a walk.'

Eleanor paused, suddenly recalling her husband's joke about getting lost. She opened the door and looked around for a lurking footman; sure enough one appeared, alerted by the sound of her bedchamber door opening.

'The breakfast parlour, my lady?'

'Yes, thank you. Am I the first or are there others down before me?' She realized that she had thanked the footman, something she was not supposed to do.

'Lord Upminster and the marquis are the only gentlemen down so far, my lady,' the young man told her with a friendly grin.

Good heavens, she thought, this breakfast parlour is the same size as our ballroom. The room was walled with long windows facing the park. Another enormous table ran down the centre populated solely by her husband

and brother-in-law. They both stood and bowed informally in her direction.

'Good morning, my love, could you not sleep, either?' Leo teased, as he sauntered casually towards her.

'Good morning, Leo. I am so glad you are here. And, as you asked, I slept very well, thank you.'

He smiled ruefully. 'Certainly better than I did. Come and sit with us. What can I get you to eat?'

Over a leisurely breakfast, Eleanor discovered the brothers were going to ride around the estate. Leo had not visited his birthplace since he had left, almost fifteen years before, to join the army and he wished to see how things had changed.

'I will ride Rufus and Gareth will take Hero. Do you want to come; there are dozens of suitable mounts in the stable?'

'No, thank you, I'm going to walk around the park, it looks so beautiful out there.' She thought of an important question she wished to have answered. 'Gareth what time is luncheon, I would not want to miss it.'

'One o'clock.'

'Will his grace come down and join us, do you think?'

Leo answered, surprised at her ignorance. 'Luncheon is only for ladies; gentlemen are expected to wait until dinner to eat again.'

'So that is why you always eat so much at breakfast,' she answered laughing.

On her return from her walk, about half-past ten, the house was still free of guests. Mary removed her outdoor wear and boots and went to hang them up. 'I will not need you for a while, Mary. I am going to explore indoors until nuncheon.'

Eleanor now recognized the route to the imposing main stairs and arrived, successfully, in the hall a few minutes later. She looked around for the friendly footman who had escorted her to breakfast.

'I would like to be taken to His Grace, the Duke of Rothmere's apartments.' If Leo would make no push to heal the rift between his father and himself, she would do it for him.

15

Eleanor wandered about the duke's main reception room wishing she could change her mind and leave, but she could hear voices coming her way.

'Who did you say, Finch? Lady Upminster? Impertinent chit, I don't recall inviting her to visit.' The irascible voice could only belong to Leo's father. She turned to face the double doors at the far end of the room. They were opened ceremoniously by two footmen and His Grace, the Duke of Rothmere, strode in.

Eleanor laughed in delight. Why, she thought, he looks exactly like Leo, including the forbidding frown. Now I know where Leo gets his bad temper from. Remembering her manners, she belatedly sank into a graceful, deep curtsy, trying unsuccessfully to hide her smile.

She introduced herself. 'I am Leo's wife, Eleanor, your grace.'

'I know who you are, girl. I want to know what the devil you mean by arriving here without an invitation?'

Eleanor straightened no sign of a smile now. 'I am sorry, your grace, if I have intruded, but I was eager to meet you because Leo has told me so much about you.'

'None of it good, I'll be bound.'

Eleanor shook her head sadly. 'No, I am afraid it was not.'

Taken aback by her frankness he asked, slightly less frigidly, 'Well, child, what did he say?'

She half smiled. 'I am not sure I should tell you, your grace, it was not very complimentary.'

'Tell me, if you please,' he commanded.

'Very well, if you insist. He said that you were the healthiest man of your age in the kingdom.' She smiled charmingly and continued, 'I suppose that is a kind of compliment. And he said that you were impervious to charm, that you would dislike me on principal and,' she counted on her fingers, 'that you had a heart of stone.'

The duke's shout of laughter echoed round the room, surprising himself as much as his two retainers, guarding the doors. 'Good God, miss, you are an original!' He smiled, his slate-grey eyes, the image of Leo's, alight with amusement. 'Come and sit with me. I wish to get better acquainted.'

Eleanor stayed with the duke until it was time to change for luncheon. The morning, she considered, had been well spent. After the meal she escaped, at last, and decided to visit the library until Leo returned.

This was on the first floor, and ran the length of the West Wing; it shelved thousands of leather-bound books. She had been there less than twenty minutes when Sir Bertram Jenkins accosted her. The amount of brandy he had consumed made him more dangerous and less likely to be open to reason.

'All alone, my dear,' he said, his eyes riveted on her *décolletage*. 'Permit me to keep you company for a while.'

Eleanor took one horrified glance at the predatory gleam in his eye and started to retreat. 'I am just leaving, sir, and I have no wish for your company.' Her voice was correct and formal, a clear indication she was not available for dalliance of any sort. Bertram refused to be denied. He lunged forward, hoping to trap her against the bookshelves. Stifling a small scream of distress Eleanor fended him off, but in the struggle a strip of the tiny roses that decorated her neckline was torn away leaving a gaping hole in her bodice.

This affront galvanized her into retaliation. She bunched her fist and punched her attacker in the eye, the force of her unexpected blow sending him staggering backwards and allowing her to escape. She ran down the library frantically searching for an exit. Halfway down she found a door, and not caring where it led to, she snatched it open and fled through it.

Outside, she was faced with a long hallway full of similar doors, none of which looked in the slightest bit familiar. She knew she must not meet anyone, even staff, with her dress torn so revealingly and had to find her own way back to her room. Her heartbeat slowly returned to normal as her fear receded and was replaced by indignation. She hoped, when she told Leo, that he would call the obnoxious Bertram out.

⋆   ⋆   ⋆

Meanwhile, a footman seeing Sir Bertram follow Lady Upminster into the library, and knowing his unsavoury reputation, raced downstairs to summon discreet assistance. Fortunately he met Lord Upminster on his way to join his wife.

On hearing who was in the library Leo took the stairs two at a time. He burst into the room just as Eleanor escaped but he saw the strip of roses still clutched, incriminatingly, in his cousin's hand. Giving Bertram no warning he grabbed his shoulder, swung him around and landed a massive blow full in his face. He followed it with several more shattering jabs to the body and with hardly a whimper, Sir Bertram, collapsed unconscious.

Still blind with anger Leo leant down and was preparing to take his wife's attacker and throw him bodily through the window, when there was a discreet cough from behind him. Leo dropped his hand and gave the butler a rueful smile, his anger under control now. 'Pity, I had hoped to pitch this object out of the window, but I suppose I must refrain.'

'Indeed, my lord, most wise. Do not concern yourself. We will clear up here.'

Leo gave Melville a half bow as thanks for his timely intervention and hurried out behind the footman, eager to find Eleanor before anyone else did. She was bound to be distressed after such an unpleasant incident.

* * *

Eleanor was glad to reach her room without meeting anyone. She hurried inside eager to remove the torn dress and wash the smell of her attacker from her person. Her maid was elsewhere and she was reluctant to ring; however discreet Mary was, the fewer people who knew about the incident the better.

In a matter of minutes the ruined dress was

discarded and Eleanor had changed into a plain, long-sleeved, primrose-yellow gingham. She tossed the torn dress into a corner, doubting if she would ever wish to wear it again. Carefully opening her bedroom door she checked the corridor was clear, then she flitted down the stairs and back into the grand salon where the ladies were taking afternoon tea.

'There you are, my dear Eleanor, come and join us.' Sophia patted the empty space beside her. 'I have just been telling Lady Whitecastle about your treasure trove of fabrics.'

Eleanor slipped into the seat and smiled at her sister-in-law. 'The gingham I used for this came from India, as well.' She smoothed the material between her fingers. 'It is a lovely colour but rather too thin for the English climate.'

Sophia laughed. 'Too thin for Rothmere, I think you mean. I do believe it is warmer outside in the stables, than it is in here.'

The tinkling laughter of the ladies was the sound that greeted Leo when he strode in moments later. He paused, his concern for his wife vanishing at the sight of her sipping tea and enjoying a comfortable coze as though she had not a care in the world. He had expected, not unnaturally, to find her collapsed in floods of tears, hiding in her room, waiting for him to comfort her.

Relieved this was not the case, but puzzled nevertheless, he strolled over to watch his wife from a distance. Eleanor felt his presence and her eyes flew to his. She saw the question there and smiled her reassurance.

'Pray excuse me; I have something of importance to discuss with Lord Upminster.' She stood up, dropped a polite curtsy, and walked over to Leo. 'I am so glad to see you; I must talk to you in private.'

'We will go to your bedchamber; we can be sure no one will wish to disturb us there.' He pulled her arm through his possessively and they left, well aware that their departure was being watched with amusement by some, envy by others, and disapproval by a few of the more senior ladies present. Unfortunately the doting aunt of Eleanor's attacker was one of them.

'Have we created another scandal, Leo?'

'I do hope so, my love; it is far too long since anything out of the ordinary happened between these august walls.' Chuckling quietly they mounted the stairs and quite flagrantly returned to their rooms hours before it could be considered necessary to change for dinner.

16

The skinned knuckles of Leo's right hand caught Eleanor's attention as they entered her room.

'You have hurt yourself, Leo.'

He glanced down, flexing his fingers thoughtfully, before lifting her similarly bruised left hand. 'As have you, my love. Shall we exchange stories, do you think?' Leo led her to the comparative warmth of the fire. 'Wait here; I will fetch some seats for us.' She shivered and coughed as an icy blast of smoke filled air belched out of the fireplace. 'God's teeth! This room is colder than a bivouac in Spain.' Leo placed two chairs as close to the flames as was safe then kicked the logs, sending sparks flying out on to the carpet. Stamping out the embers warmed them up nicely.

Eleanor viewed the selection of holes left in the rug, with horror. 'Oh dear, now look what has happened. We have ruined this priceless Persian rug.'

He was unrepentant. 'Serves them right for allowing your fire to die down. Now the new logs have caught it will soon warm up.'

'Monk's Hall is so much warmer,' she said pensively. 'Being a duke is not really as much fun as I imagined.'

They settled companionably beside the roaring blaze and for a while neither spoke. 'Leo, I am sorry but Sir Bertram tried to kiss me whilst I was in the library and I am afraid I punched him in the eye.' She glanced across to see how her unladylike behaviour had been received by her husband. After all she had promised to behave with decorum.

Leo, smiling slightly, collected her damaged fist and raised it slowly to his lips. His touch sent a surge of heat pulsing round her body. She wanted to snatch the burning hand away but could not. Sensing her disquiet he released her. 'A worthy injury, my love, and I am proud of you.'

'You are? I am so relieved; I was sure you would be angry. I know I should have fainted and screamed for help but I was so incensed I had to punch him.'

'So did I, my dear. I think Bertram will not forget his visit to Rothmere.' He grinned, stretching out his legs towards the fire. 'I was going to throw him out of the library window but unfortunately Melville stopped me.'

'Leo! How dreadful! It is fully thirty feet to the ground; you would have killed him.'

'If he touches you again, I will do so.' There

was no trace of amusement in that statement.

'Then I am glad he has left. But you must try and remember you are no longer a soldier, Leo; you must not consider killing everyone who annoys you.'

He chuckled at her gentle scolding. 'I promise, sweetheart, I will not kill anyone if you promise not to put yourself in such danger again?' His words were spoken humorously but his meaning was clear. Eleanor shuddered but managed a weak smile.

'I promise. Are all husbands so blood-thirsty, or is it your military background that makes you so fierce?'

'Even Gareth, the mildest of spouses, would kill, without hesitation, anyone who had the temerity to offer injury to his beloved Sophia.'

'Good heavens!' She thought a little then nodded. 'Well, it is hardly surprising, I suppose, for you and Gareth are brothers after all.' There was a tap at the door and Mary came in.

'I beg your pardon, my lord, lady; may I light the candles and draw the curtains?'

Leo nodded. He stood up yawning widely. 'I will leave you to change, Ellie. We are dining early tonight. Guests will start arriving for the ball at nine o'clock.' He smiled down at her. 'Are you looking forward to your first dance?'

'Yes, of course. Will I be able to waltz, now I am married?'

He frowned. 'Only with me, Ellie, no one else.'

'I have no wish to waltz with a stranger. But may I dance cotillions and quadrilles with other partners?'

'I have no objection to that for I will certainly not be doing so. Do you have your dance card?'

Eleanor handed it to him and in bold black scrawl he pencilled his name against the three waltzes. 'Get your maid to call me when you are ready to go down.'

'There is no need. I can find my way without getting lost.'

'I will take you down, Eleanor.' Surprised by his vehemence she nodded. The door closed behind him and she felt Mary relax.

'Are you wearing the green silk tonight, my lady?'

'I am, Mary. I know emerald is an unusual choice for a first ball but it is such a beautiful gown and I doubt I will have an opportunity to wear it again, anytime soon.'

By ten minutes before six o'clock Eleanor was ready. Mary arranged the flowing skirt of the first real ball gown Eleanor had owned. 'I swear that dress is the exact same colour as your eyes, my lady. I never knew you had so much green in them.'

Eleanor leant over to examine herself. 'Neither did I, I always think them more brown than green.' She pinched her cheeks and compressed her lips hoping to add some needed colour. There was a soft knock on the communicating door. 'Come in, Leo. I am ready,' she called loudly, quite forgetting that a lady never raises her voice. 'I have decided to wear the emeralds Aunt Prudence left me, they are a perfect match for this gown.'

Leo strolled in, an exasperated smile curving his mouth, prepared to take her to task. The words congealed in his throat. Could this beautiful stranger be his Ellie? The woman standing proudly before him, literally, took his breath away.

His eyes narrowed dangerously as they travelled slowly down her lustrous dark hair, arranged on top of her head and crowned with a circle of sparkling green gems, to the low *décolletage* that emphasized her breasts and gave tantalizing glimpses of their smooth white curves. His eyes raked the length of emerald silk, down to her toes, peeping beneath the hem, in matching dancing slippers. The half train, spread out around her feet, made it appear she was standing in a shimmering pool of green.

He stepped forward, still without speaking, until he was so close they were sharing their breath. She swayed towards him and his arms closed round her, holding her close to his pounding heart. His lips brushed hers in a gentle, tender caress and she was lost; her limbs turned to liquid and if he had asked she would have lain with him then, and given up her chance to attend the ball.

'Ellie, darling, you are so lovely. I have never seen a woman so beautiful.' Somehow Leo forced himself to step back, to drop his arms and move away from temptation. 'Now is not the time, my sweet. But, if you are sure, then I will come to you tonight, after the ball.'

Eleanor felt heavy with a tension she did not fully understand, but she knew only Leo could give her the release she needed. 'I will be waiting, Leo, I hope you do not disappoint me.'

Startled, his eyebrows raised in shock. His bride was an innocent, what could she know about such things? He was about to ask exactly what she had meant but the moment was lost. 'Come, Leo, I can no longer hear people going down. I do not wish to be late, especially not tonight.'

Mary quickly opened the door and they

swept through, Leo having his wife's arm tucked firmly into his.

★ ★ ★

Lord and Lady Upminster arrived for dinner at precisely five minutes to the hour. They were so lost in each other that they failed, at first, to notice the danger flickering in the air. Leo halted, and appeared almost to sniff, like a wolf sensing its prey. He stared down the long room to the tall man, leaning elegantly, in a pose exactly like his own, against the mantel shelf.

It was then Eleanor realized she had forgotten to inform her husband she had already made the duke's acquaintance. Leo walked stiffly, his face expressionless, towards the father he had not seen for almost fifteen years, taking Eleanor with him. He halted and bowed formally.

'Your grace, may I present my wife, Eleanor?'

'How are you, my dear? I see you have not mentioned to my son that we have already met.'

She smiled enchantingly. 'I am so sorry, your grace, I completely forgot.' To the astonishment of the assembled spectators, His Grace, the Duke of Rothmere, roared with laughter.

'Well, that has put me nicely in my place.' He smiled at his son. 'Leo, I have much to say to you, but I prefer to do it in private. Will you come to the study with me?'

'It is six o'clock, your grace,' the marquis reminded his father.

'Then dinner will be late tonight. Will you come, my boy?' His eyes implored Leo to follow, to take the first step to reconciliation. Leo looked from his wife, smiling innocently, then to his father, waiting hopefully.

'I will come, your grace.'

Eleanor watched the two tall men walk away together knowing that at last her husband could put his past behind him and learn how to be a happy man. If he was content then, of course, she would be too. Total silence followed the departure of the duke and his youngest son. Sophia stepped across to Gareth, her face anxious.

'It is all very well for his grace to say dinner can be delayed this evening, but what about the hundred guests arriving at nine o'clock? We can hardly leave them seated outside in their coaches whilst we finish our meal.'

'You are, as usual, quite correct, my dear. We will not delay dinner.' Gareth turned decisively to the butler, Melville. 'Have something sent in to his grace and his lordship, will you?'

178

Melville spoke quietly to a footman and then moved towards the door that led into the state dining-room. Two flunkies flung open the doors and he announced loudly. 'Lords, ladies and gentlemen, dinner is now served.'

Gareth and Sophia headed the queue and the rest fell in behind. Eleanor found herself on the arm of a young man with an extravagantly high collar and a violet silk waistcoat. Her eyes gleamed with barely concealed amusement as he tried to turn his head to talk to her.

His conversation was so vapid she was relieved when he abandoned the attempt and sat, pink-faced, staring straight ahead, for the rest of the elaborate and interminable meal. Sophia led the ladies out, not for tea, but to retire to their rooms to adjust their hair and smooth their gowns, ready for the ball.

Sophia found Eleanor waiting, rather forlornly, on her own. 'Come, my dear, the first guests are arriving and I want to introduce you to everyone. You look wonderful; you have been receiving envious glances from several ladies already. There are will be a stream of them demanding to know who your dressmaker is before the evening is out.'

'I wish Leo would return; he is pencilled in for the opening waltz, and if he is not here, I will be obliged to sit it out with the debutantes.'

'Remember, my dear, Leo and his father have a lot of years to cover, a lot of bad feelings to bury. That cannot be done in five minutes.'

Eleanor sniffed. 'I know that, but they have been closeted together for almost three hours; I cannot imagine what they can still have to say to each other after so long.'

Gareth joined Sophia and Eleanor on the stairs, and the depleted reception line was ready to greet the first of their guests. For the second night in a row Eleanor was forced to bob and bow, smile and nod, to far too many total strangers. By the time the orchestra struck up she was exhausted and almost glad she was not to stand up for the dance.

She watched as Gareth led his lovely wife to the centre of the room to stand, poised, under the row of glittering crystal chandeliers. The conductor raised his baton.

'I believe this is my dance, my lady?' Leo bowed, and offered his hand; his eyes met hers and inexplicably her gown seemed too tight. Unable to speak, she placed her hand in his and allowed him to lead her out to stand, as was his due, beside his brother.

The music started and Leo slid his arm around her waist and drew her close, far closer than was seemly. With her free hand resting against his chest he swept her away in the dance of love. Like all Wellington's staff officers he had been obliged to dance, but unlike some he moved with a lightness of step that belied his size.

Eleanor believed she was flying as he twirled her around; gradually other couples, including Gareth and Sophia, stood back to allow them to glide, as one, from end to end of the vast ballroom. They made a striking pair. Black and emerald intertwined. The young women sighed, wishing they had such a handsome husband, but the young men just watched, knowing they were outclassed. Only the dowagers muttered sourly that the behaviour of some young women left a lot to be desired.

The most vicious tongue of all was the aunt of Sir Bertram Jenkins. Her darling nephew had been doubly assaulted by the pair spinning round the hall. Then he had been sent packing and banned from ever visiting Rothmere again. She leant confidingly across to Lady Whitecastle sitting beside her. 'My dear Lady Whitecastle, did you hear that Lady Upminster met Sir Bertram in the library?'

Lady Whitecastle, an inveterate gossip, prickled with interest, anticipating a choice and tasty morsel was coming her way. 'Surely you are not suggesting that Lady Upminster made an assignation? She is a new bride and so obviously in love with Upminster.'

'It is not always as it seems. I know my nephew should not have gone to meet her, but he is young and susceptible; how could he refuse to meet such a beautiful young woman?'

Lady Whitecastle stared searchingly at the young woman smiling up radiantly at her husband as he led her from the floor. Lord Upminster bowed and kissed his wife's gloved hand then turned and strode off to join his father for a game of billiards.

Instantly Eleanor was surrounded, like bees around a honey pot, by eager young men wishing to claim her for the next dance. Eleanor took the hand of one and allowed herself to be led to a set forming at the far end of the ballroom.

Lady Whitecastle turned back. 'Pray continue; what transpired in the library?'

'Well, the young hussy flirted outrageously and allowed herself to be kissed. However when she saw her husband enter she screamed and pretended she had been accosted.'

Lady Whitecastle's face paled and her eyes turned again to the lively young lady spinning down the room, drinking in the attention of every besotted young man. 'Good heavens, what did Lord Upminster do?'

'He attacked poor Bertram and knocked him unconscious. He then had the servants evict him from the premises.'

'Why did he not protest his innocence, explain what had happened?'

'How could he? He is a gentleman. He would never besmirch a lady's reputation, however well deserved.' Her poison spread; Bertram's aunt finally noticed Sophia sailing towards her, an ominous expression on her face. 'Please excuse me, I see someone I must speak to.'

Sophia glared after the woman's rapidly retreating back. 'What did she want, Lady Whitecastle? Was she spreading slander about my sister-in-law?'

'Of course, I do not believe a word of it, everyone knows what a bounder her nephew is.' But Sophia had detected a certain coolness in Lady Whitecastle's glance as it rested on Eleanor, blissfully unaware of the storm about to engulf her.

Eleanor's thoughts, when she had the

breath to think any, were of the night to come when the man she loved would make her his true bride.

* * *

By the time the last waltz was called the gossip had spread and inevitably Leo overheard the lies as he was heading for the ballroom to claim the last dance with his beautiful, desirable wife. Two young men, who had not been lucky enough to claim a dance with the beguiling Lady Upminster, were discussing what they had heard. Leo was standing behind them, scanning the ballroom for his wife.

'Do you think it could be true? What they are saying about Lady Upminster?' Leo stiffened, bristling with anger; how dare these whippersnappers discuss his wife?

'That she agreed to meet Sir Bertram and it went sour? No, I do not. It is malicious rumour and best ignored.'

Leo had been reaching forward to grab the shoulder of the speaker but at the young man's words he dropped his hand and pushed forward. His brusque, 'Excuse me', caused the two men to wilt visibly and vanish into the press of people surrounding the ballroom. They knew the punishment that had been meted out to Bertram and did not wish to receive the same.

Leo saw his beautiful bride, radiant, surrounded by attentive young men, and the poison settled into his heart. Insane with jealousy, he strode across the room, his face hard and cold.

17

'I believe this is my waltz, Eleanor?'

She smiled and looked up at Leo. Her stomach plummeted. What had she done to anger her husband? Whatever it was, it was bad, very bad.

She curtsied. 'Yes, my lord, it is. But if you will excuse me, I am too fatigued to dance again, even with you.'

Leo nodded, the epitome of politeness. 'Then I will escort you upstairs, after you have made your adieus.' Eleanor placed her trembling hand on his rigid arm and allowed him to lead her down the line of tabbies watching, sharp eyed, from the gilt chairs at the side of the ballroom.

She curtsied, nodded and murmured her good nights, a fixed smile pinned to her face. Only Sophia was able to detect her fear and see Leo's anger.

It was approaching one o'clock and Mary was dozing by the fire when they entered. Before she could speak, Leo dismissed her summarily. What he intended to say to his wife was not for a servant's ears.

Eleanor wanted it over, whatever it was.

'Well, my lord, what am I supposed to have done this time, to so displease you?'

Leo let his eyes trail contemptuously up and down his wife but didn't answer. She flushed under his stare and anger stirred. How dare he look at her like this? She had done nothing to be ashamed of, whatever he might believe. She glared back, her fear replaced by indignation.

'I am waiting, my lord.'

His eyes narrowed at her defiance and his iron control began to slip. 'You might well ask, Wife; I was under the impression I had married an innocent but now I know I have been deceived.'

For a moment Eleanor was too shocked to speak. Her husband was accusing her of something so awful she could not bear to name it, even to herself. Leo took her silence as proof positive of her guilt. 'So this is why you have been denying me my rights? You knew I would discover your deception if I shared your bed.'

Eleanor erupted, common sense and calm discussion were forgotten as her hurt burst out. 'How dare you accuse me of such foul behaviour? You are despicable. How I ever thought I could be happy with you I cannot imagine. Get out of my room. Your presence makes me sick.'

Leo recoiled. Had he been mistaken? Her anger appeared to be genuine. His lovely young wife turned her back on him in disgust and he knew he had ruined any chance they had ever had of having a real marriage.

The girl he had married had turned into a woman and had rejected him, and his unjust accusations, totally. He paused for a moment longer wishing his intemperate words unspoken, cursing his temper and his jealousy. He remembered how they had planned to pass the night and knew, by his unforgivable error of judgement, he had denied himself, perhaps for ever, the pleasures of the bedroom.

Eleanor heard the click of the door as it closed behind him and her shoulders sagged. She stumbled across to the bed and collapsed; her eyes remained dry but her heart was in pieces. She lay there listening to the last carriages leaving and heard the silence of the night reclaim the house. Wearily she sat up, stiff from lying still for so long. She knew what she must do; she had to leave Rothmere, leave her husband, and find shelter somewhere faraway, where he could never find her.

Decision made, she felt better, stronger, ready to take back her life from Lord Upminster and become the independent, unencumbered, person she had always wished to be. She grabbed the bell-strap and pulled it gently. Mary would have to organize the packing and alert John. The carriage would need to be ready. Eleanor knew if she didn't make her escape before anyone else was up she would be stopped; especially if either Leo or Gareth heard about it.

'Is there something wrong, my lady, I thought you were abed?'

'We are leaving, immediately. When I am changed you must go down to the stables and tell John to put the horses up. I am going to ride Rufus, so have him saddled as well.'

Mary shook her head but wisely refrained from comment. 'Will I pack some food for the journey, my lady, as we won't be waiting for breakfast?'

'If you can, Mary, but only if the kitchen is unoccupied. I do not want anyone to alert the household.'

The trunks were packed and John and two grooms crept up the back stairs to collect them. By the light of the full moon and with the frost crisp under foot, Eleanor slipped, shadow like, from a servant's entrance and headed for the stable yard.

'The baggage is aboard, my lady; I'm sorry but it was necessary to place some of it inside.'

'Is there still room for Mary?'

'Yes, my lady, and for yourself, if you wish to travel inside, later on.'

'Excellent. Then we must leave, I want to get a distance between Rothmere and us before anyone realizes we have gone.'

John tossed her in to the saddle and jumped on to the box. The candle lamps were lit on each corner but their light was dim and without the full moon they would have been obliged to travel in darkness. The subdued procession trotted out of the yard and took the tradesmen's route behind the barns. Leo, standing morosely at his bedroom, staring across the park, saw and heard nothing of his wife's departure.

★   ★   ★

After a ball no one would be expected to rise before noon. Breakfast, for those who required it, would be served in their rooms. Melville and his army of servants would have the great house to themselves. By the time the first guests drifted downstairs everything would be immaculate, no sign of the previous night's revelry apparent.

Leo had abandoned any hope of sleep and at seven o'clock rang for his man to bring him water to shave. As the sky turned pearl grey and the first ribbons of pink appeared, he headed for the stables. He needed a gallop to clear his head. John was nowhere around, which was odd, but a Rothmere groom appeared when he called.

'Yes, my lord? Shall I saddle Hero for you?'

Leo hesitated; should he take Rufus this morning? 'Yes, please. Is John not about?'

'Shall I see, my lord? I expect he is having his breakfast.'

'No, saddle Hero. I will speak to him on my return.'

Two hours later it was full light, but the sun had no warmth and the park was still white. Leo had achieved his aim; he was exhausted and ready to sleep. He returned to his room, almost knocked on the door of Eleanor's chamber, but refrained: she needed her sleep. Time enough to try and repair the damage he had done when they were both rested.

He half smiled as he sat for Sam to remove his mud-spattered boots. It was Christmas Eve; when Ellie saw the presents he had for her maybe she would begin to forgive him. He would beg her pardon, explain how he had come to make such a mistake, and pray the spirit of Christ's birth would allow her to take pity on him.

* * *

'My Lord, wake up, wake up. His grace is here, and wishes to speak with you.'

Leo was instantly awake. 'Let him come in, Sam. Don't keep him standing outside.' Leo leapt out of bed. He snatched up his brocade dressing-gown and barely had time to tie the belt before his father burst in.

'Eleanor has gone, Leo. What in God's name did you say to her last night to cause her to bolt?'

Leo strode across to the communicating door and flung it open; his father was mistaken, Eleanor was in her room, as she should be. The room was empty, the bed unslept in, and Leo finally realized, in that instant, that he loved his wife: that Eleanor was the most important thing in his life and without her he would merely be existing, not living.

As the enormity of his loss sank in, he slumped against the door frame in despair. His stupidity and filthy temper had driven Ellie away. It was no more than he deserved; he was not a fit partner for her. He straightened; glad now the marriage was in name only. It would have to be annulled; he would set his little bird free. She could have Monk's Hall and he could go to the devil.

Wallowing in his misery he had been ignoring the duke quietly standing beside him. A firm hand on his shoulder shook him back to the present.

'Get after her, my boy; it is never too late. That gal loves you and when she has calmed down she will be ready to forgive you.'

'What is the point, your grace? I accused her of being impure! I realize now, I must have been insane with jealousy to speak such nonsense. I cannot ask her to forgive me; my position is irretrievable. I am going to get the marriage dissolved. It is all that is left for me to do.'

The duke was astounded. In spite of their estrangement he had followed his younger son's career with interest and knew Leo was a man of courage. 'I have never heard such drivel. What are you thinking of, boy? If you love the gal, fight for her.'

'I do not deserve her, Father. She is too good for me.'

'Poppycock! You are the equal of any woman in this country. Your birth is impeccable and so is your fortune.'

'I have no money, your grace, apart from the funds from Aunt Prudence.'

His father shifted uncomfortably. 'Not so, my boy, not so. I released your dear mother's estates to you years ago, and confirmed the title to you.'

'What? Why was I not told of this? God

193

damn it! I would not be in this mess if I had known.'

'From what young Eleanor told me, my boy, if you did not wish to see the estate in some wastrel's hands to gamble and drink away, you had no choice, either of you.'

Leo scowled at his parent. 'I would have been marrying for Ellie's sake, not my own. Good God!' Leo's face cleared miraculously. 'Of course, the money means I can put things right. I can give her Monk's Hall and all Aunt Prudence's funds. Thank you, Father, I apologize for my incivility.'

The duke laughed and slapped Leo, hard, on the back. 'Forget it, boy. I have. Now time is passing; you must leave immediately. The sooner you sort things out with your young woman the better.'

'I do not expect her to forgive me, but at least I can give her what she truly deserves, her independence. Even as a chit of a girl she vowed she had no wish to marry and become any man's chattel.'

'Stuff and nonsense, my boy. Eleanor needs you as much as you need her. Give her a little time, she will come round.'

'I pray that you are right. Now, please excuse me, your grace, I have things to organize.'

Less than ten minutes later Leo, mounted

on Hero, thundered out of the yard, Sam close behind. They were travelling light, the baggage would have to find its own way home.

★   ★   ★

'You must go in now, my lady, it's getting light. You have been too long in the saddle.'

'No, John; I prefer to ride; Rufus will see I come to no harm.' She leant down and knocked on the coach window. Mary lowered it, her face anxious. 'We should be at Monk's Hall in less than an hour, Mary. I am riding ahead to warn them of our arrival.'

Eleanor gave neither John, nor Mary, time to protest. She urged her mount forward into a canter and disappeared down the road. She knew the way from here; she had ridden this way often over the years. Rufus's long raking stride ate up the miles until he could smell his stable. Without waiting for permission he broke into a gallop and Eleanor grabbed a handful of his flying mane to steady herself.

They raced down the drive and clattered to a halt outside the Hall. Eleanor dismounted with difficulty, finding that her legs were weak, for a moment she needed to hang on to the saddle to steady herself. 'Stand, Rufus.

Wait here. I am going to knock.'

She hobbled up the marble steps and hammered on the door. She heard Brown's footsteps as he headed in her direction. There followed the sound of the bolts being drawn.

The door swung open slowly. Brown's mouth dropped. 'My . . . my lady, we did not expect you.'

'Of course you did not, Brown. Please get someone to take Rufus round and see to his needs. I require a hot bath prepared immediately and something to eat. I am sharp set for I have eaten nothing since supper yesterday.' She gave her instructions briskly as she entered, allowing Brown no time to question her about Leo. 'And Mary and the luggage will be here shortly. See that there is someone to greet her and take care of things.'

'Yes, my lady, at once.'

She paused on the stairs. 'Have the tray sent up with the bath; oh, and send Smith to me.' Aunt Prudence's abigail was, since her mistress's death, semi-retired but would, no doubt, enjoy the challenge of making Eleanor respectable.

The tray of coddled eggs and crispy fried ham, with fresh bread and home churned butter arrived before her bath was ready. Eleanor wolfed it down. Every joint and muscle ached and groaned after her exertions and she sank into the hot bath with a sigh of pure pleasure.

For a few moments she relaxed and allowed the heat to seep into her weary bones, easing her stiffness and warming her chills. Her eyes flickered and closed and she began to drift into welcome oblivion.

'My lady, you must not sleep in there, you could drown.' Smith's anxious voice jolted Eleanor from her dreams.

'I will get out now, Smith. I am so tired I can scarcely keep my eyes open.'

'It is hardly surprising, my lady. I cannot believe that you rode all the way from Rothmere.' She enveloped Eleanor in a warm towel as she spoke, realizing Lady Upminster was too fatigued to even dry herself unaided. Like a child, Eleanor allowed herself to be draped in a warm flannel nightgown and led to her bed. She stretched out, feeling the warmth from the sheets soothing her tired body.

She had attended a ball, stayed up all night and then ridden for hours: it was no wonder she was exhausted. She snuggled down gratefully on to her goose-down mattress, knowing she could sleep for a couple of hours only, if she was to be gone before her husband arrived. Her party had made excellent time but Leo was a soldier, he would travel even more quickly.

Whilst Eleanor slept, the staff at Monk's Hall, organized by Brown, carried out her detailed instructions. Boxes of books, pieces of furniture, clothes, carpets and food were found and packed into an open cart and a coach. John, the grooms, and Mary were also enjoying a few well-earned hours of sleep.

Brown, once appraised, by Mary, of the reason why her ladyship had arrived so unexpectedly, was efficiency personified. He might be a stickler but he, like the rest of the staff, loved the new Lady Upminster, and he would break all the rules to see her safe from that rogue she had been forced to marry. At two o'clock precisely, Mary woke Eleanor with a hot drink and a tray of scones baked specially for her.

'It is time to go, my lady. Everything you asked for has been done. The coaches are ready outside. Two maids, two footmen, plus the two grooms and Tommy, the stable boy, as well as John, Smith and myself, have agreed to accompany you.'

'That is wonderful news, Mary. I still ache all over. It is a good thing that I am travelling inside today. I am sure I would fall off if I tried to ride.' She yawned. 'Do you know if Rufus is still sound?'

'John said he is as sound as a bell. He ate

his fodder and drank a bucket of water and is eager to be off again. It is a pity you have decided to leave him behind.'

The staff had assembled, haphazardly, in the entrance hall to wish their young mistress farewell. Only Brown was privy to the secret of their destination and Eleanor knew he would never reveal it.

Tears glistened in her eyes as she left the house she loved, knowing she could never return. She took her jewellery and all the money she had been able to find. Taking the gold Leo kept in the study safe for expenses, had felt like thieving, but she knew she had no choice. Where she was going every penny would be needed if she, and her small party, were to survive.

18

Leo could hear the bells ringing out to celebrate the birth of Christ as he galloped through the moonlit countryside. He and Sam had already stopped briefly to rest their mounts and slake their thirst. For the third time he slowed his desperate pace and allowed Sam to catch up.

'How much further, do you think, Sam? You are a better judge than I.'

Sam stood in his stirrups and, taking his eyeglass from his saddle-bag peered over the fields towards the distant sound of bells. 'That's the bells of Lampton, my lord, if I'm not mistaken.' He sat back and, folding his glass, returned it to the bag. 'That means we have another ten miles, no more. We should be there in an hour.'

'Good, I pray we are in time.' The two men relaxed, sharing a pasty and a few swallows of watered wine. The heavy breathing of the horses accompanied their meal.

Sam handed the flask back to Leo. 'My lord, forgive me for asking, but why are you so desperate to reach Monk's Hall? What is it you fear could happen there?'

Leo gathered up his reins and shoved his feet back in the stirrups. 'She will not stay at the Hall, Sam. She will go elsewhere and then I might never find her.'

'Not find her, sir? She will not travel alone, surely? A coach or two and a chestnut stallion should not be hard to track. Don't despair, we have found smaller targets before this, haven't we?'

'You are right, and Ellie, and her entourage, will be safely asleep when we arrive. I am worrying unduly.' He clicked at Hero and galloped off into the night and Sam had difficulty keeping his master in sight.

Leo had expected the house to be in darkness. Why were the lamps lit outside at one o'clock on Christmas morning? His mouth was dry as he vaulted from the saddle and ran up the steps. The door swung open as he raised his fist.

'Good morning, my lord, we were expecting you.' Brown greeted him, his words polite but his tone unfriendly.

'Is Lady Upminster here, Brown? Tell me, man, is she here?'

'No, my lord, she is not. She departed several hours ago. I have no knowledge of her intended destination.'

In his rage of disappointment, Leo threw

his gloves and whip across the hall. 'God damn it to Hell! Sam, we are too late, she has gone.' The despair in his voice caused the butler to frown.

'Do you require refreshments, my lord, before your bath?'

Leo didn't answer. He strode across the hall and headed for the library. 'Sam,' he shouted, 'bring two bottles of brandy.' He was too late; he would drown his despair in alcohol; being drunk, the misery of his loss would be less painful.

Sam hurried after him. 'My Lord, Colonel; we will find her, but you need to keep a clear head. Be ready to leave at dawn. Getting foxed will help no one.'

Lord Upminster glared at his batman, his fist bunched and Sam braced himself for a blow. 'Get out of my sight, damn you! When I require your advice I will ask for it.' The door slammed in Sam's face and he heard the sound of clinking as brandy was poured liberally into a glass.

Two decanters were emptied before Leo managed to sink into an alcoholic doze. Whilst he snored, stretched out in a chair, his travel-stained garments steaming in the warmth of the fire, Eleanor's sad party stopped for breakfast in a deserted clearing, deep in the heart of East Anglia.

The horses were unharnessed and hobbled, canvas buckets of feed were tied over their heads and water was tipped, from one of the barrels on the open cart, into a canvas trough.

Eleanor and Mary found privacy in the dense trees for their relief while Smith helped the young maidservants and a footman set up a table and chairs for their meal. The air was crisp and cold, the ground hard, which had made their journey a trifle easier. The roads Eleanor had elected to use were often little more than farm lanes and so their progress, necessarily, had been slow.

'John,' Eleanor called her head groom over. 'We will rest here for an hour. Make sure the men rest and take refreshments also.'

'Yes, my lady. We have made good time, in spite of the going, and should reach Wenham before dark.'

'Thank you, John. It is hoped the young man you sent ahead has already arrived and warned the staff to have things prepared for our arrival.'

'Matthew is a good lad, my lady, and the horse he took is sound. He will have travelled at twice our speed; the staff at Wenham Manor will have had several hours' prior warning.'

'Come, Mary, I see the food is set out. I have no appetite, but as Smith has gone to such trouble, I will try to swallow something.'

'You must try, my lady. You don't want to fall ill now, do you?'

The food, on wooden trenchers, was simple. Slices of cold game pie, homemade chutney and yesterday's bread. They washed it down with the same water the animals drank. Eleanor's face was drawn, dark shadows hollowed her eyes. Mary was worried about her.

'Happy Christmas, Mary. It is hoped the brightness of Christ's birth reflects a little light on our sorry undertaking.'

'Happy Christmas, to you, my lady. I'm sure things will turn out for the best. God has a hand in all our lives; all we have to do is listen.'

Eleanor smiled sadly. 'It is not the Christmas I expected. But I do thank God that I have my health and my friends to sustain me.' She stood up, shaking the crumbs from her crumpled green velvet travelling dress. 'How well have we covered our tracks, John, should anyone be searching for us?'

'Well enough, my lady; we have avoided towns and villages and have put a good many miles between us and Monk's Hall. Doing our travelling at night means if we were heard, no one would have seen us.'

'Now it is daylight, we are bound to be spotted; there will be workers in the fields soon.'

'No, not today, my lady. Don't forget it's Christmas Day; most folks have the day off. The fields will be empty.'

'Excellent! For I doubt that any labourer would ever forget the spectacle of a travelling chaise, a carriage and large cart, followed by two outriders, passing by.'

The journey unwound and her new home drew nearer. Eleanor sat up and began to take notice. The flat fields stretched out on each side of them, their monotony broken by small forests and woods. She was going to miss the rolling hills that surrounded Monk's Hall. The cavalcade had passed several hamlets and she was horrified at the dilapidation of the housing.

'Mary, look at that, the roof is sagging and a stream appears to run straight into the cottage. How can the landlord leave his tenants in such misery?'

'It does look poor around here. Much worse than home — Monk's Hall I mean.'

The nearer they got to Wenham the worse the condition of the cottages. The hedges were overgrown and the fields poorly husbanded. Something was badly wrong. She knew the problems caused by unscrupulous land agents of absentee landlords, as she had read countless pamphlets on the subject, but she had never seen such blatant neglect.

'Mary, I fear this is going to be far worse than either of us anticipated.'

'We will manage, Miss Ellie, don't fret yourself. There is little that can't be put right with a lot of hard work and willingness.'

'And a lot of money, Mary, which we do not have.'

'We will manage; just think of what we experienced on our trips abroad. If we survived that we can survive anything. Isn't that right, Smith?' Mary appealed to the elderly lady half asleep in the corner of the carriage.

'Oh, yes, quite right. Whatever the short-comings of the staff and premises there are enough of us to put things right.'

'I hope you are correct. I will never return to Monk's Hall, not while Lord Upminster is in residence.'

The three ladies lapsed into silence, each busy with their own thoughts. Smith, glad she was to be of use again, Mary, praying matters would not be as bad as they feared, but Eleanor, however hard she tried, could not eradicate the darkly handsome face of her husband. She knew his behaviour had been unforgivable, that he had an ungovernable and unpredictable temper, but in spite of his many faults, she still loved him.

She had made her choice and now she would have to learn to live without him. She was grateful they were married for this meant she would never have to share her life with another man. If she could not have Leo then she would have no one.

As they trundled nearer their destination Eleanor mentally reviewed their finances. The jewellery, some purchased in India, some inherited from her aunt, should fetch several hundred pounds, if she could find a buyer in such a godforsaken part of England. She calculated the £115 in gold coin and the £20 or so in silver and bronze should be sufficient to see them through until John could find someone in Norwich to take the jewellery.

She gazed out of the window at another row of ramshackle rough cottages, its occupants too idle, or too dispirited, to come out and stare.

John raised the lid in the roof and called down. 'Matthew's riding back to meet us, my lady, he should be here in five minutes.'

'I hope he brings good news. Can you see if he looks happy, John?'

'No, my lady, he has his hat pulled down low against the biting wind. Shall I stop?'

'Yes, I will get out and talk to him.'

Tommy, the stable boy, acting as groom, scrambled down from the box and removed the folding steps and set them out. Eleanor descended and her bonnet was whipped from her head; only the ribbon round her chin restraining it.

'Goodness, it is so much colder here. The wind is so sharp and is that snow I can see in the fields, John?'

'It is, my lady. We are a good deal further north than Monks Hall, it is bound to be colder; here is Matthew.'

The young man, his face invisible under his muffler, reined in beside the stationary vehicles. He dismounted nimbly and, removing his hat, came over. He was grinning. 'The Manor is in some need of repair, my lady, and understaffed because no one has been in residence for years. But the housekeeper, and the few girls she has, appear to be delighted you are coming. She has had some rooms cleaned and fires lit; you won't be displeased with your welcome.'

Eleanor unclenched her fists. 'Thank you, Matthew. Is it much further? Will you lead the way?'

'Mile or so, no more.' He swung back into

the saddle and trotted off to lead them to Wenham Manor.

They did not pass the village of Wenham, it was on the far side of the Manor, but they did pass several rows of rundown cottages that were, Eleanor was relieved to see, not in such gross disrepair as those they had seen earlier.

It was just then they turned through the rusty lopsided gates and bowled along the weed — infested drive. The trees hung darkly across their route and cut out the remaining light. The carriage, after travelling in darkness, finally emerged into the fading light and Eleanor had her first glimpse of Wenham Manor. Every window was filled with welcoming light, the imposing front door stood open and the elderly housekeeper waited on the steps to greet them, her face creased with smiles.

In the excitement, and relief of their arrival, Eleanor failed to notice the broken shutters, peeling paintwork and slipped tiles. She stepped into the stone-flagged entrance hall flanked by a beaming Mrs Bacon and three smiling, bobbing maids. She stopped enchanted by the sight that greeted her. The hall had been decked with holly and ivy and red ribbons had been pushed amongst the branches. An enormous, sweet-scented, yew log, burnt in the cavernous grate. The whole was lit by hundreds of candles.

'Oh, look at this, Mary. It is so lovely. What a wonderful welcome.' Impulsively she grasped Mrs Bacon's hands. 'Thank you, Mrs Bacon, I shall never forget the trouble you have taken today.'

'It were nothing, my lady. It is Christmas after all; it were lovely to have the excuse to decorate the place how it should be. Now come on in do, your chambers are all ready, and there's a hot bath waiting for you. I'll not show you up meself, a lass can do it, I'll get back to the kitchen. I have a Christmas meal cooking for you; it will be served in the dining-room in an hour, if that is acceptable?'

'That will be wonderful.' She smiled at the girl waiting to escort her to her new rooms. 'Come along then, show me the way, I need to see my new accommodation.'

The girl led the way up the wide central oak staircase. It led to a gallery which overlooked the entrance hall. 'This way, if you please, my lady. Your rooms are at the back; they face the park and get the sun in the morning.'

Eleanor and Mary walked behind. The runners were threadbare but the wood was polished and there was no sign of neglect inside the Tudor building. The girls stopped in front of an ornately carved door. 'Here we are, your ladyship.' She opened the door and stepped back to allow Eleanor to precede her.

The room was large and square; mullioned windows filled the far end; an enormous oak bedstead, piled high with feather mattress and comforter, stood centrally, and on the right, opposite the bed, a roaring fire blazed merrily in the grate. In front of the fire, screened from the window draughts, stood a large hip bath. The lemon-scented water drew Eleanor towards it.

'Thank you, my abigail can manage now.' The maid dropped a curtsy and vanished through a cleverly concealed door in the wall, to the right of the fire.

'This is very acceptable, Mary. And it is considerably warmer than the room I used at Rothmere.'

'Indeed it is, my lady.'

A banging and bumping could be heard on the other side of the panelled wall. Eleanor looked at Mary with astonishment. 'Have we noisy ghosts here, do you think, Mary?'

'Oh, my lady, I hope not!'

There was a loud knock on the hidden door. Eleanor laughed with relief. 'It is the trunks arriving. There must be a passage running behind that wall.'

Mary hurried to the door and the two footmen staggered in, trunks balanced on their backs. 'Put them there, boys. You may leave the rest outside; they can come up tomorrow.' Red-faced and puffing, the young men retreated, glad they did not have to manhandle any more boxes up the narrow stairs and maze of dark corridors that made up the servants' route. Mary locked the door behind them. 'Now you can take your bath, my lady, and I will sort out your garments while you do so.'

Downstairs, Smith had taken it upon herself to play the role of housekeeper whilst Mrs Bacon was preparing their meal and had allocated rooms, and bedding, to each of the indoor staff who had travelled with them.

John found dry stabling for the tired horses in a derelict building and temporary accommodation for the two grooms, stable lad and himself in a cluttered room above the animals. Eleanor had thoughtfully included palliasses and warm blankets in the cart so no one would have to sleep on the boards.

* * *

The heavy oak table in the dining-room groaned under the weight of food set out for Eleanor. She sat in solitary splendour and forced herself to try a morsel of each lovingly prepared dish. The housekeeper came in to see if the meal had been enjoyed.

'Thank you, Mrs Bacon, that was truly delicious. You have made what I expected to be a miserable Christmas Day, into a happy occasion.'

'You be very welcome, my lady. It's a true pleasure to have a mistress in residence after so long.'

'Please make sure all the staff share in the feast. I will require nothing else this evening. I hope you will be able to enjoy your Christmas meal without interruption.'

Eleanor was escorted to her chamber by Smith. It helped having familiar faces serving her, but the strangeness of the mansion, with its low-ceilinged reception rooms and heavy black beams, seemed to be weighing her down.

Mary removed her gown and slipped a warm flannel nightdress over her head. 'I have warmed the bed, my lady, and the commode is behind that screen. Will you need anything else?'

'No, Mary. Go and enjoy your meal. I am sure I will sleep tonight; I am tired after all the travelling we have done.' But her feather pillow was saturated with tears long before she finally fell into a deep, dreamless sleep.

19

The rattle of the bed hangings being drawn back woke Eleanor. 'Good morning, my lady; it is nine o'clock and I know you don't like to sleep in.'

Eleanor rubbed her gritty eyes and yawned. If she had slept so long why did she still feel so exhausted? 'Put out my divided skirts, and heavy boots, Mary. I wish to explore my new home.'

'But it's Boxing Day, my lady. None of your tenants will expect a visit so soon.'

'More reason to go then. They will have no time to hide from me. I want to know why the estate is in such disrepair. I remember Uncle George telling Aunt Prudence, when she inherited Wenham Manor, that it was a veritable goldmine. So why is it so poor now? I need to know what has happened here.'

'As you wish, my lady.' It was Mary's tone which alerted Eleanor to her folly. It was hardly fair to descend on her tenants on one of their few day's respite, however eager she was to get answers.

'You are right, Mary. I will concentrate my attention on the Manor and grounds today. I

214

am sure there is plenty here to occupy me.'

Mary, who had already ventured outside and seen the parlous state of the house and outbuildings, felt it only fair to warn her mistress. 'I fear you are in for a nasty surprise. John says the stables and barns are all but falling down and I noticed several places in this roof where the tiles are missing.'

'As bad as that?' Mary nodded. 'I cannot understand how this has happened. Where has all the revenue gone, for it certainly has not arrived at Monk's Hall? I only knew Wenham was still part of the properties once owned by Aunt Prudence because I found the deeds hidden away in the back of the safe, when I was looking for money to take with us. It was then that I realized Wenham Manor was the perfect place to go.'

Mary's eyebrows disappeared under her cap. 'I can't believe it! Where were you intending to take us then?'

'I have no idea, Mary. I just knew we had to get away from Monk's Hall. It was the hand of God that led me to those deeds, it must have been. I was praying hard enough for a solution.'

'Well, I'm glad that He did, or we would still be wandering around in the cold like lost sheep.'

The vast flagged hall was gloomy and the

greenery looked less attractive in the puddles of weak sunlight that had managed to find its way through the leaded casements. The yew log was still burning fiercely in the grate and she was glad of it. Even with several layers of wool she was finding it hard to keep warm. She stared around; the vaulted ceiling and massive carved oak stairs, flanked by lopsided suits of rusty armour, the dark panelled walls, the axes and shields from a bygone age hanging above the fireplace, gave the hall a heavy, old-fashioned feeling.

Smith, dressed in black, appeared from a dark passage on the far side of the stairs. 'Good morning, my lady, shall I direct you to the small dining-room?'

'If you would. I need to speak to Mrs Bacon as soon as I have eaten. Ask her to join me in the library.' She stopped and shook her head. 'Is there a library, Smith?'

'Yes, there is. There is also a study, which is smaller and, if you don't mind my saying so, it is much warmer than the library.'

'Then I will use the study, thank you, Smith.'

By midday Eleanor had established herself firmly as the head of the household. She knew where the most urgent repairs were needed and where the most skilled artisans were to be found. She also confirmed Smith as housekeeper, and Mrs Bacon as cook. John was next on her list. He arrived in the study incensed by what he had discovered.

'Sit down, John. Tell me, just how bad is it, outside?'

'Bad, my lady, very bad. A new roof is needed at the stables and the barns are so ramshackle it might be best to pull them down and start again.'

'Will it be expensive? Funds are short, as you know.'

'The five of us can do most of it, and if we use salvage it shouldn't be too dear. But the outbuildings are not the worst of it. I hardly know how to tell you what I have discovered.'

'Go on, John, I have to know what I am facing.'

'Very well, my lady. The land agent, Anderson, who took over from his father when he died a few years back, is a nasty piece of work from all accounts. He evicted the rightful tenants and cottagers and installed his own family and friends in their place. The poor cottages we passed had been condemned by old Anderson. They are now occupied by the displaced people. They had nowhere else to go. The Poor Rate is all most of them have to live on. It's a disgrace, that's what it is. The houses are not fit for pigs, let alone a family with little ones.' It was the longest speech Eleanor had ever heard him make.

'And I suppose the illegal tenants are dwelling in well-kept homes and young Anderson is living like a lord at my expense?'

John nodded. 'That's the right of it, my lady. The village is divided; those who have benefited from Anderson's corrupt practices support him, and the others are against him.'

'I will call him here, and dismiss him. Then I will appoint a new estate manager and put things back as they ought to be.'

John hesitated, not sure it was his place to speak. 'Forgive me, but it isn't as simple as that, my lady.'

'Why? I am the mistress here; it is my right to appoint and dismiss staff.' Her voice became less certain when she saw John's expression. 'It *is* my right, is it not, John?'

'Not in law, my lady; this property is owned by Lord Upminster now and Anderson does not have to take orders from you unless told to do so by Lord Upminster.'

Eleanor dropped her head into her hands. The only way she could intervene in the running of the estate was with her husband's support, and that she would never apply for. She straightened; she had to make the best of what she had.

'Will there be any problem if I employ the

displaced cottagers?'

'I doubt it. The Manor and its grounds are within your domain, it is the farms and tenants you have no jurisdiction over.'

'Then that is how it will be. John, I wish you to become my man of affairs. Is there one of the under-grooms who can take your place in the stables?'

He stood up and beamed. 'Thank you, my lady. I will not let you down. Young Matthew Jeffries is ready to take my place as head groom. I will draw up a list of what needs doing. May I return with it later?'

Eleanor agreed. She sat pensively studying the notes she had made. There was so much work to be done to restore this lovely old house and so little money available to do it. She had no one to talk to about her concerns. Mary, John and Smith were both literate and numerate but they were still her employees, not her equals. This was a burden she had to bear herself.

★   ★   ★

The Twelve Days of Christmas passed and the festive evergreens were removed. Bereft of its finery, the empty hall looked bleak and unwelcoming.

'Smith, have you sent anyone up to search

the attics yet? Is it possible that there are still other treasures stored away up there?'

'I'm afraid not, my lady. What there was has gone out to John, to furnish the rooms above the stable. It was nothing of any worth.'

Eleanor was puzzled. She understood her aunt and uncle had never resided at Wenham Manor but Lord Dunstan had visited several times and his glowing description of the interior did not match what she found.

'I would like to see Mrs Bacon, now.'

A few minutes later a tentative knock on the door heralded the cook's arrival. 'Sit down, Mrs Bacon. I have questions that need an answer.'

Mrs Bacon paled at Lady Upminster's formal tone. 'I will help in any way, I can, you know that, my lady.'

Eleanor leant forward, her eyes narrowed. 'Well, tell me this, if you please. What has happened to the furniture, rugs, paintings, silver and plate that belonged to Wenham?'

This was the question Mrs Bacon had been dreading. She wiped her eyes ostentatiously on her snowy white apron. 'Oh dear, my lady, it was awful. When old Mr Anderson, God rest his soul, passed on, his son took over and he is a black-hearted villain. He stripped the house of everything of value and there was nothing I could do.' She wrung her hands piteously. 'How could I stop a man such as him?'

Her fine performance did not fool Eleanor. Her voice dripped scorn when she answered. 'Why did you not contact Lady Dunstan immediately?' Mrs Bacon shrank into her seat. 'I will tell you why, Mrs Bacon, because you are in league with him. You are dismissed. I want you away from here before dark, or I will have John throw you out. Do I make myself clear?'

Mrs Bacon's obsequious manner vanished instantly. She jumped to her feet, her face contorted with rage. 'You will regret this, my girl. Mr Anderson will have you out of here. Everyone knows you are here because Lord Upminster has banished you, because you are a disgrace to his good name.'

'Get out of here. Remove yourself from my sight.' The raised voices had attracted the attention of Smith and the two footmen. Eleanor was relieved to see them. 'Smith, this person is to leave Wenham Manor instantly. She will take nothing with her. She will not return to her room. See her out of the gates.'

'Yes, my lady.' Smith replied, her face stern. The two footmen grabbed the flailing arms of the once pleasant cook and dragged her, heels kicking, from the room. Her screams of abuse and wild threats echoed behind her.

Eleanor sank back into her chair, trembling uncontrollably. Had she done the right thing? Mrs Bacon had seemed so plausible, so pleasant and welcoming; why hadn't she seen it was a façade masking a dark and vicious nature? She heard heavy footsteps approaching the study and quailed. Surely it wasn't the hated Anderson, here so soon, to extract revenge?

John, his face shocked, appeared in the open doorway. 'Is everything all right, my lady? It should never have happened. It is my duty to see to such unpleasant matters. Why didn't you call me?'

'Thank you, John, I am almost recovered, but I am glad to see you. Do you know that wretched woman has sold all our furnishings? I suppose this means the three girls are also in with Anderson?'

'It would seem likely, yes. I think we must have them in here, in turn, and see where their loyalties lie.' He reached over and pulled the bell-strap.

Smith appeared almost instantly, looking flustered. 'Oh, my lady, I was just on my way. What a to-do there has been. The three girls have all gone as well. I never hope to hear such language again!'

John looked serious. 'That answers our question, my lady. We are better off without them; all inside people have to be trustworthy.'

'We cannot run this house with so few staff; we have no cook and no kitchen maids now.'

John stood up. 'I think I know how to solve that problem. I've employed several men from the cottages and know there are women down there equally desperate for employment.'

Eleanor relaxed a little. 'Send someone down to ask. We need a cook, and three girls for general duties.' She looked across at Smith, worried double duties might prove too much for the elderly spinster. 'What about gardeners and outdoor people, John?'

'The park grounds are overgrown and the kitchen garden is more weeds than vegetables. Four men could make a start on righting things. Unfortunately we have no accommodation for them; they will have to work at day rates.' This meant, Eleanor knew, that they had to be paid, in cash, at the end of each working day. Live-in staff were paid monthly, or even six-monthly, in arrears. A better proposition for someone as stretched for funds as she was.

John went off to search out the extra staff and Smith to organize the clearing of the rooms occupied by the four women who had left. Eleanor felt overwhelmed by the responsibility and worry. She had always wanted to be independent, to run her own affairs; it was only now she was discovering just how difficult this could be for a woman on her own. She began to appreciate why most left such matters to their husbands and concerned themselves exclusively with domestic issues.

The women who arrived just before dark were a pathetic sight. Their garments were so patched and worn it was hard to tell what colour they had originally been. Eleanor left the selection to Smith and John. She knew she would find it hard to turn anyone away, even the most unsuitable of the candidates.

Dispirited and lonely, she wandered through the sparsely furnished house and wished she was back at Monk's Hall. Tears rolled, unbidden, down her cheeks. Her life was in ruins. She was a wife, with all the restrictions and none of the advantages. Had she been too hasty in judging Leo? Had she once again acted impulsively and landed herself in a situation she was not capable of solving? Too miserable to eat, she retired to bed and for another night cried herself to sleep.

★ ★ ★

Leo had woken Christmas morning with a head like a bear-pit and a mouth to match.

Sam was unsympathetic and was, Leo felt, unnecessarily noisy as he moved about the room. 'What time is it, Sam?'

'Past midday, my lord,' was the terse reply.

'Hell's teeth! What can I have been thinking of?' Leo swore. 'The trail will be cold by now. We should have set off at dawn.'

'Yes, my lord.'

'Sam, do you wish to remain in my employ?' Leo asked smoothly.

Sam scowled. 'I am not sure that I do, sir.' This unexpected answer jolted Leo out of his post-drunken daze.

'Good grief, Sam, you do not mean it, do you? I know I have behaved badly, but not so beyond the pale that you wish to quit?'

'Can I speak plain, my lord?'

'Yes, go on, man.'

'You married the best young lady any man could hope to find; you were as happy as a lark in her company, and then you threw it all away in a fit of jealousy.' He paused, his face contorted with worry. 'Where has the little lass gone, my lord? How will she manage out there on her own, with no one to protect her?'

'And if any harm comes to her, it is all my fault? Thank you, Sam, you are absolutely right. You are telling me what I already know.' Lord Upminster swung his legs on to the floor and stood; wincing, he grabbed the bedpost as his eyes blurred and his stomach revolted. 'Now is not the time to leave, Sam, I need your help. We have to find Eleanor. I cannot do it speedily enough on my own; will you help me, please?'

It was rare that the colonel said please to anyone under his command. 'Very well, I will not make a decision until I know Lady Upminster is safe and well. Then I will decide.'

Leo dressed quickly, not prepared to wait for Sam to assist him. He had not adopted the skin-tight unmentionables and Weston coats that needed two men to pull them on successfully. He shrugged into his comfortably fitting navy-blue superfine and pulled on his Hessians. He was focused and ready for action. He had lost a skirmish but the real battle was yet to be fought.

He ran downstairs with Sam at his heels. He had letters to write. He was recalling his troops for action. If he was to locate his wife it was going to take more than Sam and himself. With good fortune on his side, within a few days, soldiers, men he had fought beside, whom he had led into battle, would start arriving at Monk's Hall.

While Sam galloped off to take the letters to the nearest post house, Leo drew up his plan. Using the maps spread out on his desk he worked out all the possible routes Eleanor could have taken if she had wished to avoid being seen. He was intending to send pairs of men down each road to search for her.

When she was found the second man could return, post haste, leaving the other to watch and wait for him to arrive. Satisfied his plan was as faultless as it could be, he sat back, kneading his neck with his fingers. The duke had been right; he would not give Ellie up without a fight.

If, in the end, however, she decided she wanted no more of him, he would release her from her vows, but he knew, of a certainty, that whatever she felt he would never be free: he would love her until his very last breath.

20

The new people melded seamlessly into the weave of life at Wenham Manor. The drive lost its growth of weeds, the rickety gates were straightened and both horses and grooms now had a rainproof roof over their heads.

All this had been achieved with a minimum of expenditure. Eleanor had not needed to dip deeply into her meagre stock of gold sovereigns. Wood from the dismantled out-buildings was recycled to repair the stables. Bricks and stones from the same source were used in the same way.

Eleanor was never happy, she believed she would never experience that wonderful feeling again, but at least her life was tolerable and for that she had to settle. Helping the destitute did give her a sense of satisfaction but it could hardly compete.

In three weeks she had seen remarkable changes. The manor house looked cared for outside, although the inside remained some-what lacking in comfort and style. She felt herself sufficiently settled to venture, with both John and Mary for support, into the village. On a fine cold morning in the middle of January she left the grounds for the first time since she had arrived.

John, smart in his new brown tweed cloth coat and black breeches and boots, sat opposite to his mistress and Mary, demure in grey worsted, sat beside her.

'I am a little concerned that our reception will not be favourable, John. From what you have heard, Anderson and Mrs Bacon have many supporters.'

'There are as many locals who welcome your arrival, my lady. You have offered hope to several families on the verge of starvation.'

'I know, John, but what about the influx of soldiers and sailors who have returned here now they are no longer needed for the war? Which side will they take?'

Mary pursed her lips. 'The side on which their bread is buttered thickest, most like.'

Eleanor chuckled. 'No doubt you are correct. Perhaps we can entice them to our side by offering them work. John, I think it is time you took my jewellery to Norwich and tried to sell it.'

'Oh, my lady, not the lovely things you got in India, and the family pieces Lady Dunston left you?'

'I am afraid so, Mary, I no longer have need for diamonds and emeralds.'

Conversation ceased as the carriage rumbled into the main, indeed the only street of Wenham village. Eleanor saw little to impress. The mean cottages they passed had patchy moss-stained lime-washed walls and unkempt gardens. The village boasted one inn, The Bull, which looked in danger of collapse, with rotten thatch and crumbling walls. There were a huddle of commercial buildings which included a general stores, a cobbler's, and undertakers. The smithy was the only premises that showed signs of life.

The duck pond was deserted of both and people and the large green was home to a few sheep and two scruffy goats. 'What a depressing place. Where is everyone? I thought at least the legal tenants would be prosperous and spending their money in the village. There is no sign of business anywhere.'

'There were plenty of folk at the inn, I noticed, as we drove past,' Mary said sourly.

John tapped on the opening in the carriage roof. A fresh young face appeared in the gap. 'Drive through and take the next left-hand lane; it will take us round and back to Wenham Manor.'

Eleanor was thoughtful on the way back. If Anderson's people were living in poor circumstances where was all the money from her farms going? 'John, can you find out where Anderson lives, and in what manner?'

'I can tell you now, my lady. He has bought a substantial property in Norwich and is living the life of a gentleman.'

'On my money? How dare he? Why did you not tell me this before?'

'There's nothing you or I can do to change things. I am sorry, I should have told you.'

'Yes, you should, John. It is scandalous. If my money was being used for the benefit of the estate then I believe I could have borne it. But not this; I will not have it.'

John was worried. He knew how unpredictable his young mistress could be. Feeling against landlords was running high in neighbouring villages. It would not take much to cause a riot; half the population were living at starvation level and they had nothing left to lose.

'I have business locally tomorrow, my lady. Perhaps we could go to Norwich the day after that, if the snow holds off?'

'That will be fine. I believe I will attempt to see Anderson, and if he is not at home, I will leave him a letter, setting out my concerns.' She smiled at Mary. 'It will be enjoyable visiting Norwich; at least there people will not be prejudiced against me.'

The return route took them past the

cottages inhabited by the farm workers Anderson had installed. Eleanor noted the neat gardens, freshly whitened walls and new thatch. She directed her companions' attention towards them. 'They are the only decent homes in this area.'

'Anderson's family and friends live in them, that's why, my lady,' John told her.

'That is something, I suppose. A man who takes care of his own cannot be all bad, surely?'

'You are too kind, my lady. The man is no better than a thief and outlaw.' John refrained from completing his sentence out loud. He had been about to say that his lordship would soon send Anderson packing, but he was sure he had not been the only one thinking exactly that.

'I have not changed my opinion, John. However, it does allow one a modicum of hope that he might be open to reason, when the time comes to confront him.'

★   ★   ★

Mary was not happy. 'My lady, I beg you, please reconsider. John says there was a violent protest in Hadleigh and the militia were called. Two men were killed and several farms were burnt before it was put down.'

232

'I know that, but as Hadleigh is more than a day's ride away I am sure we are in no danger. I have no intention of causing a disturbance. I am merely going to visit Anderson. I will have John, a coachman, and two grooms with me. I will be quite safe. The man is corrupt, not a vicious outlaw.'

Mary accepted defeat. 'If you must go then I am glad that I will be accompanying you. It would not be right for a lady to go alone to a bachelor establishment.'

'I have asked John to have the carriage brought round at eight o'clock. It is a good two-hour drive to Norwich and we might well be delayed by poor roads and other traffic. It is a blessing it will not be a market day.'

Eleanor had dressed carefully for her confrontation. She wanted to appear confident, and in control, and considerably older than she actually was. The russet-brown walking dress and matching pelisse were smart but not frivolous. It had only two braid ruffles around its plain hem. The small poke bonnet she selected was unadorned apart from two matching ostrich feathers. A pair of dark-brown kid half boots, completed the outfit.

Satisfied she presented a businesslike appearance Eleanor was ready. She was not relishing the thought of meeting Anderson but believed she had no choice. Injustices had been committed and as the landlord in residence it was her role to put them right.

John handed her up into the carriage and Mary followed. He climbed in and banged on the roof with his cane. Matthew, the coachman, with Tommy, the stable boy, beside him gave the matching greys the order to move. The two grooms rode behind, stout cudgels clearly visible behind their saddles.

The weather had stayed cold and the rutted lanes were passable. But no amount of springs and padding could fully insulate the occupants from the jolts and drops of a country lane. As Eleanor's bonnet shot down over her eyes for the second time she smiled.

'I suppose we should be grateful the going is hard. If it was wet we would no doubt be stuck every five minutes, instead of tossed about like shuttlecocks.'

Mary carefully restored the offending bonnet to its correct place on Lady Upminster's head. 'I hope the roads improve soon, John; we are likely to be black and blue long before we reach Norwich.'

'We will be turning into the main route soon, things will improve then, I promise.'

The jouncing and bouncing and constant need to adjust her hat and her hair at least had the benefit of taking Eleanor's mind from her forthcoming encounter.

The carriage and its outriders trotted into Norwich a little before eleven o'clock. The city was thick with traffic and loud with the noise of traders shouting their wares and the clatter of horses and wheels on the cobbles. The carriage stopped in front of an imposing, solid, brick residence setback from the road, at precisely noon.

Eleanor peered from the window. 'Is this it, John?'

'Yes, my lady. I will go and announce our arrival.'

She sat back; her heart thudded uncomfortably and her stomach roiled. She was glad they had not stopped for refreshments. She watched John walk up the steps to the front door and bang on the ornate brass knocker.

The door was opened by a black-uniformed maid. It was impossible to hear what was being said from that distance but it was certainly not the news they wanted. The door closed and John returned to the carriage.

'Anderson is not at home. It appears that he is visiting relations in the country today, the maid said.'

'Do you think she is telling the truth?'

'Yes, I am sure of it.'

Eleanor shook her head with annoyance.

235

'We should have discovered whether he would be at home before we set off.'

'Then he would have been forewarned of our visit. It was a risk we had to take. Shall I take the letter, my lady?'

'Yes, I have no choice. I would have much preferred to have spoken its contents to his face, than have him read of my displeasure and intention to wrest back control of the estate.' She delved into her reticule and handed it over. 'Now, Mary and I can visit the shops. John, you must take the jewellery and get the best price you are able. We will meet, as arranged, for tea, by the castle. Afterwards I hope you will have substantial funds to deposit in the bank.'

The carriage turned round in a nearby park and threaded its way back to the centre of the town.

★   ★   ★

All the participants in the excursion were well pleased with their afternoon. John had sold the jewellery for a substantial amount and had opened an account and safely deposited the banker's draft. The two grooms had imbibed two tankards of excellent porter and devoured several tasty meat pasties. Tommy had been perfectly content left at the ostler's to mind the carriage and the horses. Eleanor, accompanied by Mary, had traipsed happily in and out of the haberdashers, milliners, and the large general stores.

Her many purchases were in boxes and bags secreted beneath Matthew's perch and also tucked neatly under the seats in the coach. Eleanor leant back with a sigh. 'Apart from missing Anderson, I consider this day well spent. I can hardly credit the amount you raised for my valuables, John. Will you organize the repair of the cottages immediately?'

'I will, my lady. At a shilling a day we can afford to employ several extra labourers. I will do as you suggest and recruit, where I can, from the ex-soldiers.'

'The plight of the working man in this area is pitiful. They do not even have the factories to find employment in, as they do further north. It is hardly surprising that there is unrest. The land owners and Parliament are to blame. They should lower the cost of corn and find work for these poor souls. Aaahh . . . ' Her political speech ended with a scream when the coach lurched violently to one side as the offside rear wheel dropped into a deep rut. The resulting imbalance rocked the vehicle, evicting its passengers from their seats.

For a moment, from her position on the floor, squashed under both Mary and John, Eleanor thought all would be well, that the coach would right itself. Then her world turned upside down as the coach toppled sideways into the ditch.

Mary cried out as her head cracked hard against the seat and was then ominously silent. John tried to brace himself, jamming his longer, stronger legs, hard on to the side, hoping he could keep his weight from crushing either of the ladies. The sound of the horses neighing outside and the voice of Matthew soothing them while the grooms expertly cut the mangled traces, brought Eleanor back to her senses. She could scarcely breathe; her slender frame was trapped beneath the unconscious form of her maid. Where was John? She prayed he was not injured as well.

A pair of strong arms gently eased Mary to one side, and allowed Eleanor to draw a shaky breath. 'Lie still, my lady.' John instructed her. 'We must not rock the coach. We are balanced on the lip of a deep drainage ditch; a sudden movement from any of us will send us plunging into several feet of icy water.'

Eleanor needed no further urging. 'Are you hurt, John?'

'No, bruised is all. Have you any injuries?'

'I think not, but I fear Mary is badly injured. What are the men doing? Will they try and right the coach or attempt to lift us out as it is?'

Matthew's worried voice answered the question for her. He spoke to them through what was now the side but had previously been the floor of the coach. 'My lady, sir, we daren't move the coach until we have it stable. I have sent Tommy to the village for help. Jess, Davey and I will tie a rope on to the wheel and then fasten it to a tree across the road.'

'Will it take long? Mary's hurt and needs urgent attention.'

'We will work as speedily as possible, my lady. But the weather is worsening and it will soon be dark. Please keep still, movement could prove disastrous.'

Eleanor began to feel cold as damp from the ditch started to seep through the side of the coach. She stared at the far door, now facing skywards; Matthew was right, it would soon be dark and the temperature was dropping fast.

The village they had driven through was no more than a mile away. Tommy should be back anytime with help. There was no need to worry; accidents were an inevitable part of travelling along poor lanes. She tried to see how Mary did, but her face was trapped against the seat. Carefully she inched her hand across and placed it on Mary's neck, the sticky dampness she discovered there filled her with foreboding.

'Mary, Mary, can you hear me? We will soon have you out of here. Please do not worry; help will be here very soon.' She received no answer, not even a whimper.

John knew he could not hold himself away from the ladies for much longer. His leg muscles had started to twitch and he could feel cold sweat forming on his brow. They both heard the sound of a galloping horse thundering back down the lane.

'Thank God,' Eleanor cried, 'we are saved. Help has arrived.'

21

Leo strode up and down the study, he had never been a patient man and waiting for news was the hardest part of any campaign. That the news he wanted would come, he had no doubt; failure was not a word Colonel Upminster had in his vocabulary. His men were not only enquiring at little villages and farms for news but also visiting towns with pawn shops and jewellers. When Eleanor took her valuables to sell, within a day, Leo would know about it.

Sam burst into the study, waving a much folded letter. 'It has come, my lord, I think Jenkins and Sharpe have found Lady Upminster at last.'

Leo took the missive with a smile of relief and scanned its contents. For the first time since Christmas Eve he felt a glimmer of hope. Then his expression changed. 'Good God, Sam, this does not look good. She is living at Wenham Manor, and about to embark on a confrontation with a corrupt estate manager.' He frowned, thinking fast. 'Send messages to all the men to meet us at Wenham. There has been civil unrest in that area already and if Eleanor stirs the pot she could find herself in the middle of a riot.'

'We can be ready to ride in an hour, my lord.'

'Good. I am glad Jenkins and Sharpe had the sense to stay put, God willing they can keep Ellie from harm until I reach her.'

He raced upstairs to change. Sam unwrapped a sword and scabbard from its protective covering of oilskin and handed them to Leo. 'You will be needing this, my lord.'

Leo's face was bleak as he strapped them on. 'I will take my pistols and you, your rifle, Sam.'

'Yes, sir, I have them here.'

They clattered back down the stairs and Brown blanched when he saw the accoutrements of war so casually displayed. He wished now he had broken faith and told Lord Upminster where his wife was hiding. If any harm came to his beloved mistress he would never forgive himself.

Hero and Rufus sensed something momentous was happening. They stamped impatiently and snorted; clouds of vapour encircled their heads. Leo vaulted into the saddle and shouted across to Sam. 'It is a bad day, Sam; I never thought to wear this sword again, or to see you carrying a rifle.'

'It is a precaution, my lord. With luck we

will have no cause to use them.' Leo not usually given to exchanges with his Maker sent up a fervent prayer that Sam would prove to be right.

* * *

Eleanor heard Matthew shouting to the rider as he approached. His words sent a chill of foreboding slithering down her spine. 'Surely you have not come alone, lad? Where are the others you went to fetch?'

'They refused to come, sir. Those that bothered to answer my knock, that is.'

'Then we'd best get on and sort out this muddle ourselves. We have the rope tied but it is not as secure as I'd like.' Matthew shouted into the coach. 'Mr Jones, sir, can you move yourself, careful mind, to the side? We need all the weight over here, if it is not to slip when we lift the ladies out.'

John knew his limbs were tired from supporting his body for so long and feared they would not obey him when he released the pressure. His reply was confident however. 'When I shout, you hang on for your lives. Now!'

The coach creaked and rocked as John slid his boots down the door until they were either side of Eleanor's legs. 'I will roll sideways as you open the door, John, which should help prevent us sliding further into the water.'

'Very well, my lady. You ready, lads?'

An enthusiastic chorus of assent rattled the windows. John launched himself against the door above his head and simultaneously Eleanor rolled herself across to join him. The coach held its position. The combined weight of three strong men clinging on to the wheels, and the rope attached to the convenient tree trunk, plus John and Eleanor inside, had served its purpose.

John had the door open in a trice, and leaning down he gripped Eleanor's arm. 'Up you come, my lady. Careful now; keep leaning hard on the side.'

Eleanor had been about to suggest that Mary be taken first but felt it prudent to follow John's instructions. She was stiff and damp and her once smart outfit was wet and clung heavily to her legs. 'I am ready, John. What do I do now?'

'If you will forgive the liberty, I'm going to lift you up and then you must scramble through the door. Ready!'

Eleanor felt John's arms around her waist and she stretched up, straining to catch the door jamb with her fingers. The coach groaned ominously and they felt it move towards the water. 'Quick now, we don't have much longer.' She felt John's shoulder under her bottom and at last her fingers found a purchase.

Grateful she was fit and slender, Eleanor, with John pushing her from behind, emerged head first through the door and dropped into the lane glad that, in the darkness, her undergarments would have remained invisible.

She came up on to all fours and regained her feet. 'I am out, John. I will add my weight to the wheel. Matthew can help you with Mary.' Her hands, in their sodden gloves, were almost too cold to function but desperation gave her the strength she needed. She prayed that she could hang on hard enough to stop the coach plunging away, carrying Mary, in her unconscious state, to a certain death.

John was working blind; he grovelled for Mary's feet and dragged her limp body slowly towards him. His eyes were wet as he bent down and transferred his hold to grip under her arms and around her shoulders. They had worked together for years, had become fast friends, but as he clasped her to his heart he realized that his feelings had somehow, without his knowledge or permission, changed. He now loved the woman he held so close.

This love gave him Herculean strength and with one heave he pushed her up into the waiting arms of Matthew. As her legs vanished through the gap the coach began its inexorable slide towards the waiting water.

Eleanor screamed as her fingers lost their grip. 'John, John, get out quickly! We have Mary safe.' They could hear the fibres of the rope tearing. It could not hold the coach much longer. Inside John braced his legs and climbed furiously for his life.

The rope snapped. The three men jumped back, there was nothing more they could do. The noise of the coach falling drowned out all other sounds. It toppled on its back and vanished into the ditch. Eleanor's voice broke as she spoke. 'Oh John, poor John, he was such a good man.'

'Thank you, my lady, and I hopes to remain a good one for some years to come.' John's head poked through the door and his body wriggled after it. Eleanor could see nothing; it was now full dark. With Mary's head cradled in her lap she shouted with relief and joy. 'John, I can hardly believe it. How can you be alive? I heard the coach tumble into the ditch.'

He thumped down beside her and she heard his boots squelch as he landed. 'It's stuck, my Lady. When it tipped over the wheels must have snagged on the under-growth and it held fast. Upside down, mind, and several inches in the water, but safe as houses it is now.'

'Thank God, for that.' A faint movement and groan captured their attention. 'Mary? Can you hear me? You are safe now. We are all safe.'

Mary moved her head and groaned again. 'I have a mortal bad headache, my lady, and am that cold, I cannot feel my feet.'

John knelt beside her. 'For a while I thought we had lost you, my love; I am so glad you are safe.' The endearment did not go unnoticed by Mary, or her mistress.

'Get along with you, John Jones. I am right as tuppence. Get up from there, you big lummox and give me a hand. I'm no good to anyone lying down here.'

The men got Mary to her feet. She swayed a little and complained bitterly about her head, but was otherwise able to move.

'We'll have to double up on the horses, my lady; if we don't get you both back, and into dry clothes, you will catch your deaths.'

'You take Mary up with you, John. I will double up with Jess and Tommy can ride with Davey. Matthew can go on ahead and lead the way.' No one argued; her instructions made sense.

'How will we even find our way home, it's black as pitch.' Mary said, through chattering teeth.

John grinned in the darkness. 'They'll find their own way, my dear; all we have to do is sit tight. Horses are sensible beasts; they will take a safe route, don't you fret.'

The horses, even with their double burden, made better progress than the carriage. Barely an hour later the sorry troop clattered into the yard. Eleanor had been hoping they would be met by a rescue party, worried at their late return. But the snow fell on to a deserted stable yard. The lanterns were unlit and the area dark and unwelcoming. Matthew's roar of disapproval bounced around the empty yard causing both grooms and workmen to appear instantly to offer their assistance. Tommy, the stable boy, was despatched to rouse the indoor staff.

John handed his precious burden down to Matthew, then vaulted from the saddle. 'Give her here, Matt, I'll take her. Smith will know how to see to her.'

Eleanor handed her reins to Jess and trudged after John, her feet and hands so cold she had no feeling in them. The servants' door was flung open and welcome light flooded the path. Smith was framed, like an elderly crow, in the light.

'My lady, I'm so sorry, as darkness fell I assumed you were staying the night in Norwich.'

'Never mind that; as you can see Mary has been injured and requires your immediate attention.' John bore Mary away upstairs leaving Eleanor alone within a circle of expectant faces. It was so hard to be the person responsible for making decisions.

She shook the worst of the mud from her skirts, then spoke to the head parlour maid, Jenny. 'Jenny, you are to assist me. I require a hot bath and a tray with soup and some bread and cheese, in my chamber, as soon as possible.'

Wearily she headed for the back stairs and met John returning. 'How is Mary?'

'Feeling a lot better now she is in the warm, my lady.'

'I am so glad. John, will you arrange for the coach and all my purchases to be recovered, at first light?'

'I will that, my lady; let's hope we don't get too much snow.'

★   ★   ★

Eleanor snuggled down, with a sigh of pleasure, and stretched her feet out to rest on the hot brick someone had thoughtfully placed in her bed. Full of vegetable pottage and fresh bread and cheese, her extremities finally thawed, she felt strong enough to review the accident and its aftermath.

Coaching accidents were common, especially in the winter, and she knew them to be lucky to have escaped without permanent injury; however the refusal of the villagers to assist them was both unexpected and deeply worrying. The unrest and dissatisfaction was obviously far worse in East Anglia than in Kent. Of the dozen or so indoor staff only four had come with them, and were therefore totally trustworthy, and outside, only five of the twenty men now employed, could be relied upon in a crisis.

She felt sick and, in spite of the brick at her toes, shivered violently. Not for the first time she regretted her rash move and wished she was safe, at home, in Monk's Hall.

The sound of a maid rekindling the fire and Jenny opening the curtains woke her next morning. Bright sunlight spilled across the floor cheering Eleanor immensely. 'Jenny, how is Mary this morning?'

'Much recovered, my lady. She would be up if Smith allowed it.'

'I will go and see her as soon as I am dressed; is there much snow?'

'No, my lady, an inch at the most. Mr John set off with two plough horses, the big cart, and a dozen or so men. I've no doubt they will be back before midday.'

'I hope so; it will be difficult without a closed carriage in this weather. It is far too cold to use a chaise.'

'I'm afraid your gown and pelisse may be ruined, my lady. Such a shame; they were so smart.'

'Do the best you can, Jenny. If they are irretrievable I am sure someone in the village can make use of them. I will wear my green corded gown and the matching redincoat today.' Warmly dressed, Eleanor left through the hidden door in the panelling. It was the shortest route to Mary's room in the servants' wing. Reassured that her maid was making a good recovery she completed her journey to the small dining-room down the narrow twisted staircase used by the staff. She seated herself at the table and waited for a footman to serve her breakfast.

The ham and poached eggs congealed on her plate. Her appetite had all but vanished over the weeks and she knew her dresses would soon have to be taken in. She drifted over to the window attracted by the pattern the sun made filtering through the tiny panes. The dusting of snow was gone and it looked almost spring-like. Eleanor wished she had been able to bring Rufus to Wenham; a gallop across the park would have settled her nerves.

The handsome clock in the corner chimed nine o'clock. A sharp tap on the door startled her out of her day-dreaming. Smith came in, her face ashen. 'My lady, terrible news.'

Eleanor felt her stomach plummet. Had Mary taken a turn for the worse? Had someone been injured? 'What is it, Smith; tell me at once.'

'Tommy has brought a message from Mr Jones. When they reached the coach they found it had been burnt to a cinder and all your belongings either gone or destroyed. Who would do such a thing, my lady?'

Eleanor guessed at once who the culprits were. The villagers who had refused to come to their aid yesterday would have known exactly where to find the coach. It was them, she was sure of it. But it would not help matters to scare her elderly servant.

'There are a lot of displaced people in the area, Smith; it was probably some of those.'

'I don't like the sound of it, my lady. Whatever sort of folk have we come to live amongst?'

'Hungry and desperate ones, Smith. Where

is Tommy? I want to speak to him myself.'

'In the kitchen, warming up. Shall I fetch him?'

'No, I will come myself.' Eleanor ran to the kitchen; she needed answers to several difficult questions. The cook and kitchen maid turned worried faces. Tommy, clutching a mug of steaming soup, scrambled to his feet. 'Sit down, Tommy; you can answer me from there.' Tommy subsided, his eyes wide, his straw-coloured hair on end. 'How far behind you are Mr Jones and the others?'

'About a half-hour, my lady. Not far. They 'ad to turn the cart and it were hard in such a narrow lane.'

'Good; did you see any signs of those who burnt the coach?'

'No, my lady, place were deserted; them beggars as done it were long gone. The coach were not even smoking, it were cold to the touch.'

This could only mean the perpetrators had followed Tommy when he went for help and attacked the coach as soon as it was safe. The thought that their desperate struggles, in the dark, had been seen by hidden robbers was not a happy one.

The situation was rapidly becoming one she did not feel confident to handle. With no coach she was trapped in Wenham, at the mercy of rioters and disaffected labourers. Her people were at risk. She had no option. She had to send a message to her husband. Whatever her personal feelings she was not putting her staff in danger. Leo would know what to do, a few unarmed, and untrained mobsters would be nothing to him after his battles on the peninsula.

'Thank you, Tommy. Send Mr Jones to the study as soon as he returns, Smith.'

Eleanor took paper and quill and prepared to compose the most difficult letter of her life. After several aborted attempts she still did not have a version she was satisfied with. She had tried formality, addressing her husband by his title, but feared he might toss it aside unread. Her letter must attract his instant attention.

Finally she decided to write as she would speak, if he were there with her.

Leo
I need you. We are in desperate straits here, the villagers have turned against us and yesterday they burnt out our coach. Anderson, the estate manager, has been stealing from Wenham Manor for years and foolishly I have threatened him. I fear he will retaliate.

Whatever our differences, Leo, I beg

*you, put them to one side and come to
me as soon as you can.*
Eleanor

She spilt sand across the page, shook it
clean and folded it, sealing it with a blob of
sealing wax. She would not trust this
important letter to the mail, she would send
Jess. If he rode post, changing mounts every
twenty miles, he could be at Monk's Hall by
midnight.

She tugged the bell rope. There was the
sound of heavy footsteps hurrying along
the uncarpeted passage. The hard bang on
the door told her it was John.

'My lady, I think we might have a serious
situation developing.'

'I know, John. I have written to Lord
Upminster asking for his assistance. I want
Jess to ride post; see he has sufficient funds
for the journey.'

Some of the tension left John's face. 'Excellent idea, my lady. I will see to it immediately.'

'Come straight back, John, I have several
ideas I wish to discuss with you.'

Jess was sent on his way, proud to be given
the chance to prove his horsemanship and
stamina. When John returned to the study he
found his mistress pacing up and down
impatiently.

'How many of the workmen can we rely on, if there is trouble, John?'

'Not all, that's for sure. I think the ex-soldiers will stick with us. There's two turned up this morning; they heard Lord Upminster's wife was taking on workers. It appears they served with his lordship and will serve you now, as willingly.'

'That is good news. Could you not find any other men who knew Lord Upminster when he was a colonel?'

'I am already doing so, my lady. They're out now rounding up any men who will be loyal to us in a fight.'

'Fight? Oh, John, I hope it does not come to that.'

'I hope so too, my lady. Lord Upminster, if he rides post as well, could be here by midnight tomorrow. I hope that will be in time.'

22

The atmosphere at Wenham Manor was tense; everybody understood the danger they were facing. It made no difference that the present incumbents were not to blame for the deprivation and hardship; rioters did not use logic and reason to govern their actions. They were motivated by desperation.

John pulled on his riding coat and tied his muffler snugly. 'I will not be gone long, my lady. I must go to the village and help to escort the men back, those that Jenkins has persuaded to join us.'

'What if everyone has turned against the gentry? You could be in danger. Would it not be better to allow this new man, Jenkins, to return with them himself?'

'If you don't mind, my lady, I would prefer to take Davey and Matthew and go and find Jenkins. I wish to make sure that everyone is within our walls, whilst there is still time.'

Eleanor was not convinced. Things were moving with a momentum of their own and she did not like the idea of being left without her right-hand man. The dust of John's departure had barely settled when she saw a group of well-mounted men cantering down the drive. They were strangers to her.

From her vantage point in the study window she watched their approach. The leader, a thickset man in his thirties, was well dressed, his companions far less so. Eleanor swallowed a lump in her throat. She knew who it was, and thought it was no coincidence that Anderson had timed his arrival to match John's departure.

She gathered her skirts and raced to the hall, shouting for help as she did so. 'Smith, Ned, Billy, come quickly. We must barricade the door. Anderson must not be allowed in.' The two footmen joined her by the front door and she stepped back to allow them to drop the massive bars across. They heard the horses halt and booted feet trample across the gravel and up to the door.

'Are all the other doors secured, Ned?'

'No, my lady, we'll do it now.' The young men vanished on silent feet leaving Eleanor and Smith to face Anderson alone. The door shook under the onslaught of hammering. Eleanor stepped back involuntarily. She waited, mute, for Anderson to speak.

'I know you're in there, Lady Upminster, and I know you're on your own. If you understand what is good for you, open up. I'm not a man who likes to be kept waiting.'

She took a deep, steadying breath. What could this bully do, apart from shout? The door between them was stout and the leaded windows too small to climb through. 'I have no intention of opening the door, Mr Anderson. What you have to say can be said from where you stand.' She heard him step back and speak quietly to his men. Then she heard the sound of footsteps walking away from the front door, towards the rear of the house. She prayed Ned and Billy had been in time.

Anderson returned to his position by the door. 'Lady Upminster, I will not harm you, or your staff, all I require is that you leave me to get on with my job without interference.'

'Your job, Mr Anderson, is to run Wenham Manor for the benefit of its tenants and villagers and to return all revenues to Lord Upminster and myself on quarter days.' She paused, allowing her words to be digested. 'These past five years you have taken the monies due to the estate. I will not allow the situation to continue.'

'Will you not? And how, pray, do you hope to stop it? I'm not answerable to you, only to Lord Upminster, and I don't see him nowhere, do I?'

Eleanor was tempted to tell him her husband was on his way but refrained, such knowledge would grant him time to prepare and might make Leo's task more dangerous. 'I have loyal men working for me and more are joining every day. Soon I will have enough to force you to comply.'

'Be damned to you then. If that is how you wish to have it, you only have yourself to blame if people get hurt. This is my estate, and I think you'll find, my lady, that its people fear me more than they wish to help you.'

Eleanor was weak with relief. He had gone and made no attempt to break in. They were safe for the moment and John would soon be back with the recruits. She ran to the window and watched the riders gallop insolently back across the middle of the lawn, sending divots flying in all directions. They left behind black holes in the grass as a dark reminder of their visit.

Smith hurried into the hall. 'My lady, it is terrible; the new staff are leaving. Those men threatened to kill them and their families if they remained.'

'Have the single men gone as well?'

'We have no one like that indoors, my lady. I don't know who has left outside.'

Eleanor shrugged. 'No doubt John will be able to tell us when he returns. You must not worry, Smith. Lord Upminster will be here the day after tomorrow. Why should there be any trouble before then? The civil unrest is not widespread and so far the only incident in our vicinity has been the coach burning. No person was attacked, only property.'

'But, my lady, Anderson has threatened to kill people if they stay in your employ. Why would he want to drive them away, if he wasn't planning something bad?'

'To make my life uncomfortable? To prove he has the power? I think you are refining too much on this. It is exactly what that man wishes. He wants me to panic, to pack up and leave, not stay and confront him.' Hesitant footfalls on the stairs made Eleanor look up. 'Mary, you should not be up. I told you to rest in bed today.'

'I heard all the shouting, my lady. I could not lie abed anymore. I have the headache, but apart from that, I'm as right as a trivet.'

Eleanor left her maid with Smith and returned to the study. She checked the hall clock as she passed; John had been gone over an hour, which meant he should be returning any minute and bringing the reinforcements with him. Knowing men who had fought alongside her husband, were out there, somewhere, made her feel safer.

Waiting patiently was not a virtue she had

been blessed with. After pacing the study for twenty minutes she decided to visit the stables. The presence of horses always calmed her.

Tommy, the stable lad, was standing on an upturned bucket brushing one of the greys that pulled the carriage. He hopped down and tugged his forelock. 'Good mornin', my lady. Matthew is away with Mr Jones.'

'I know, thank you, Tommy. I have come to see how the greys do, after their experience yesterday.'

'They's fine, my lady. None of the beasts have gone lame.'

'Good, carry on then, Tommy. I do not wish to hold up your duties with idle chatter.' The boy scrambled nimbly back on to his perch and resumed his rhythmic strokes.

Eleanor, restless, wandered along the boxes, stopping and patting each occupant. She had reached the last stall when she heard the men returning. Outside, in the cobbled yard, John dismounted, well satisfied with his morning's work.

'John, I am so relieved that you are back. Anderson came here with his bullyboys and threatened the new staff and they have all walked out, apart from Cook.'

John came to stand beside her, his kindly face wrinkled with concern. 'I should never have left you, here alone, my lady. It will not happen again.'

'It is not your fault, John. He timed his arrival precisely. I'm not going to fret about it. Lord Upminster will receive my letter today and, God speed, he will be here by tomorrow night.' She tensed as booted feet could be heard approaching the stable yard.

'It is not them returning, my lady. It is the new men; we have found a further ten who are more than willing to fight to protect their colonel's lady.'

'How many does that make altogether, John?'

'Seventeen in all, eighteen if you count the stable boy.'

'Will that be enough?'

'I'm sure it will. The twelve new men are soldiers, trained to fight. Do I have your permission to open the gun room and arm them?'

'Of course you do.' They walked back together towards the Manor. 'It is a good thing we repaired the gate and filled in the holes in the wall. Is it closed now?'

'It is, my lady. I have put Jenkins, Lord Upminster's man, in charge. I know little of battles and such; my life has been spent with horses.'

'That is a sensible idea. Lord Upminster's

men must be schooled in such matters.' They reached the door and John opened it for Eleanor. 'I forgot to tell you, Mary is up; she insists she is well, but I sent her to sit down with Smith. Perhaps you would like to visit with her?'

He beamed. 'I would that, my lady. It wasn't till I thought I might lose her that I understood how my feelings for her had changed. Mary and I have always been firm friends, but now we have moved on.' A pink flush stained his neck; he was unused to speaking of such delicate matters.

Eleanor stretched out and patted his arm. 'Your love for each other is good news, John. I can assure you it has my full and delighted approval. I always believed you two would be ideally suited.'

She returned to the study, for she felt there was something she should be doing, some preparation she should make, but could think of nothing. All she could do was calculate, repeatedly, the earliest possible moment she could expect to see her husband at Wenham Manor.

★   ★   ★

Jess galloped into the yard at the Queen's Head and an ostler leapt forward to take the post horse's bridle. He had ridden through the night, the full moon making his journey less hazardous. He needed to relieve himself, then break his fast, before resuming his journey to Monk's Hall.

He walked stiffly around the back of the stalls seeking the necessary privacy. As he refastened his breeches he overheard two ostlers talking, on the far side of the wall. 'That chestnut brute is a handful, Ned. I'm right glad his lordship took the feed in himself.'

'The grey is nearly as bad. He's been in the wars, a real battle horse; did you see the scars on his neck?' Their voices faded as they moved away. Jess was already racing round to confirm his suspicion. He ran down the stalls glancing inside each as he passed.

'Rufus, you old devil!' The chestnut head swung round at the familiar voice and he whickered a greeting, then resumed the more urgent task of filling his vast stomach. Jess had no idea how Lord Upminster came to be at the Queen's Head, it was nothing short of a miracle, and it would save him from several gruelling hours in the saddle. He got out the letter, written by Lady Upminster, and tried to smooth out the worst of the creases. What should he do? Wait by the stalls until Lord Upminster appeared or seek him out now?

Leo swallowed the last mouthful of roast beef with a sigh of pleasure. 'That was an excellent meal, Sam. Will you be ready to ride in a half-hour?'

'Yes, my lord.'

They both looked across at the altercation taking place by the door. A travel-stained groom was attempting to gain entry to their private parlour and not succeeding. Two burly potmen blocked the entrance.

'Lord Upminster, Lord Upminster, I have a letter for you.' The shouted message from the struggling young man caused Leo to leap to his feet. Who could possibly know his whereabouts and wish to deliver a letter to him?

He strode across and gestured to the potmen to stand aside. 'Let him in, if you please.' The men stood aside and he was astonished to see a groom, who had accompanied his wife to Wenham, step forward brandishing a grubby missive. 'Your lordship, I have a letter from Lady Upminster.'

He snatched the paper and tore it open. His face blanched. 'It is worse than we thought, Sam. The situation must be desperate if Lady Upminster is asking for my help.' His smile was harsh as he pushed the paper inside his coat. 'We leave at once. Jess, is it not?' The boy nodded. 'Are you riding post?' The boy nodded again. 'Good; engage your mount and ride with us.'

The nag, the ostler had waiting for Jess, did not meet with Leo's approval. 'Have you nothing better? This lad has to keep up with us, on that animal he will be left behind.'

The man thought. 'There is my Betty, my lord. She don't look much, but she can keep going all day without flagging. I'll fetch her for you.'

'Good man.' Leo slipped a coin into the waiting hand. The ugly bay cob that was led out did not, at first, fill him with confidence. Then he noticed the solid legs and deep-set chest and realized the horse had stamina. He made a decision. 'Will you sell the horse to me?'

'Two sovereigns, my lord, and she is yours.' The money changed hands and the men mounted. Leo turned to Jess. 'That is a good beast, Jess, I believe she will keep up, but let her find her own pace. No matter if you fall behind a little.'

'Very well, my lord. Am I not to change horses at the next post house, then?'

'No; Rufus and Hero can gallop all day, if

they are allowed to rest every twenty miles or so.'

Jess stared down at the bay he sat astride. Leo laughed at his expression. 'Have faith, lad. I know my horses. That mare will see you home in one piece, I promise.'

Jess, reassured by his lordship's confidence, grinned back and the three men clattered out of the yard, determined not to delay any further.

$\star$ $\star$ $\star$

Eleanor pushed aside her untouched luncheon. She hated eating on her own. Before she had been elevated to the aristocracy she could have taken her meals in the kitchen, along with the staff, but such familiarity was no longer permissible.

The sound of men shouting outside and running feet in the passageway made her glad she had not eaten. Her stomach lurched unpleasantly. What was happening? Were she and the staff in danger? She ran to the door and it opened as she reached it.

John, his face concerned, was outside. 'We've had a message from the cottages, a mob is heading this way. They have burnt two farms already. I fear we are next on their list.'

'Will the soldiers be able to prevent them

from entering the grounds?'

'For a while, yes, my lady. But we cannot protect all the boundaries; eventually, if they are determined to get in, they will succeed.'

Eleanor felt even sicker. 'I do not understand, why should they wish to harm us here? I have done so much to help the dispossessed and the unemployed; if they destroy us then their plight will be worse.'

'I'm afraid a mob does not think so sensibly, they have a madness on them, and collectively behave in a manner they would never do alone.'

'If we offer them food, money, or work, will they be appeased?'

'I doubt it. Someone is whipping them into a frenzy; sending them in our direction. I suspect Anderson is behind it.'

'But how will destroying Wenham benefit him? He will lose his income.'

'Not if it is only the manor that is destroyed; I fear he means to get you out, my lady, by any means.'

'Oh, I wish Lord Upminster was here, he would soon send them packing.'

'No more than I do. If we can hold out somehow until nightfall then it is just possible he will be here. The letter Jenkins sent will have reached him yesterday; he will be on his way by now.'

'Then I need not have sent poor Jess to fetch him?'

'No, my lady, it appears not. But we did not know Jenkins was working for Lord Upminster and had already sent word when Jess left, did we?'

Another hour snailed by and there was no sign of the threatened mob. Eleanor could see the soldiers armed with shotguns and pistols, patrolling around the house. Jenkins had obviously decided that protecting the boundary was a lost cause and would spread his men too thin.

As dusk was falling Eleanor heard a noise that chilled her to the bone, the mindless screaming of a mob calling for blood, anyone's blood. The maniacal chanting seemed to be coming from all around the park. How many were there waiting to destroy her home? From the noise they were making it could be hundreds. What hope did the twelve soldiers and six servants have against so many?

John hurried in. 'Stay away from the windows, my lady. It will be best if you went upstairs and locked yourself into your bedchamber.'

'I will not hide like a rabbit, when you are all outside, fighting for your lives.'

'Very well, I will leave the footmen armed

in the hall; I'm going out to join Jenkins and Matthew.'

'Take care, John.'

The door closed behind him leaving Eleanor alone with her fears.

23

Mary joined her mistress in the study. In spite of the danger, and John's instructions, they both peered out either side of the window, hoping to see what was taking place. After the initial burst of activity it was eerily silent.

'Where is everyone, Mary, can you see?'

'It's hard to see anything through the little panes.'

'But they do give us extra protection; even if the rioters smashed the glass the lead frames will hold them back.' This was small comfort to either of them. 'Let us hope it never comes to that. Maybe the mob has gone elsewhere to cause destruction.'

Mary pointed. 'Over there, look, Miss Ellie, I can see our men running towards the gate.'

'Does that mean we are under attack? I have to know. Please go up to the attic; the view from there will be clearer, you will be able to see over the trees.'

'I will, my lady. But stay out of sight; you know John said we were not to stand near the windows.'

'I am not staying here, I am going to the

kitchen, to check the doors are bolted and barred.'

Eleanor found the kitchen staff huddled miserably by the fire. No shiny black stove graced this antiquated house. All cooking was performed on trivets and spits that swung in and out over the blaze. It was an inefficient and hot way to prepare food but at least the room was warm.

The cook, the only local woman who had not deserted them, scrambled from her position on a stool beside the fire, upset by the unexpected and unwelcome visit. The further the lady of the house kept from them the better; it was the likes of Lady Upminster the mob wanted to drag down, not working people like herself.

'My lady, no one heard you ring; did you need something?'

This less than welcoming statement made Eleanor suddenly aware of the gulf that separated her servants from herself. She was not wanted here. 'I am sorry to intrude. I wish to check if you have all the doors securely fastened.'

The cook's expression changed to apprehension. 'No, my lady, I don't believe we have. Quick Bess, you go and lock the pantry door and Ellen you take the little lass and bar the back door.'

Eleanor left them to secure their side of the house. She knew Smith and Mary had been sent to fasten all the windows and the side door that led out the garden, but she needed to check for herself. If Cook had forgotten such a simple precaution then so could Smith. It was up to her to try all the doors herself. The task would also occupy her time which was welcome. The windows were as they should be, also the massive front door.

Eleanor had just reached the side door when she thought she heard someone outside calling her name. She opened the door a fraction, surprised it had not been locked. There, she heard the voice again.

'Lady Upminster, Lady Upminster. Come quickly, Mr Jones has been injured. You are needed in the stables.' Eleanor believed the voice belonged to Tommy, and he sounded frantic. She knew he would not call her unless it was very urgent.

She ran upstairs to collect her cloak and change into her stout boots before returning to the side door. She contemplated running to the kitchen to tell them she was going out for a moment, but she heard the voice again, more insistent, more high pitched. She had no choice, if John needed her she had to go, whatever the risk.

She closed the door behind her and ran

down the path to the stables, dreading what she would find. In her hurry to go to John's assistance she had forgotten that the side door was still unlocked, leaving its occupants open to attack if any members of the mob managed to evade the circle of armed watchers.

Breathless, Eleanor rushed into the stable yard to find it inexplicably deserted. Then she heard a moan coming from the end box, the unoccupied one. With thudding heart she hurried across and pushed open the half-door. A still, male form was crumpled on the straw at the far side, under the manger.

'John, what have they done to you?' As Eleanor bent over to touch the unconscious man she heard a slight noise behind her and then her world disappeared in smothering black as a thick blanket was tossed over her head and hastily secured by strong ropes.

She couldn't breathe. She couldn't scream for help. Her nose and mouth were filled with the noxious smell from the filthy cloth. She felt rough hands securing her arms and legs within its enveloping folds. Slowly she was overcome by the lack of air and merciful darkness took her away. Her body slumped out of the grasp of her attackers.

'My Gawd, 'ave we kilt 'er? Mister wanted her alive.' The swarthy, unkempt villain dropped to the straw and reached a dirty hand up under the blanket. ' 'Er 'ands are still warm. I reckon she fainted, is all.' He grabbed her slumped form and, with the help of his accomplice, heaved it over his shoulder. 'Come on, let's git out of 'ere, before anyone misses 'er.'

The kidnappers, mission accomplished, vanished with Eleanor into the empty woodlands that bordered the stable block. The noise from the mob, ranting and shouting at the front gate had provided a perfect diversion, keeping all the manor's men occupied whilst they captured Lady Upminster for their master, the estate manager, Mr Anderson.

★ ★ ★

Eleanor woke an hour later to find herself hog-tied and dumped in a corner of an evil-smelling, mud-floored shack. The single window was shuttered and barred, the door firmly closed. The ropes around her body prevented her from moving. But at least her head was now uncovered and she could breathe more easily.

How could she have been so stupid as to allow herself to be lured into such an obvious trap? Her head ached, and her mouth was full of disgusting bits of blanket. She tried to spit them out but her mouth was dry and spasms of pain contracted her stomach. She rolled sideways and tried to curl up her legs to ease her suffering, but the ropes were too well tied.

She retched, miserably, on to the floor. The sickness stopped the cramps and removed the blanket pieces from her mouth. Unfortunately the foul taste left behind was worse. She attempted to wriggle sideways, to remove herself from the mess she had made. When this failed she tried rolling but the smell of the beaten earth floor was so bad she gave up the struggle and resumed her painful sideways shuffle.

Slowly the cracks of light faded from the window and her prison sunk into darkness. The cold and damp seeped through her cloak and, two hours after her capture, Eleanor began to shiver uncontrollably. Her teeth chattered and shudders rippled up and down her body.

An icy wind whistled through the cracks in the walls and it was then she realized what Anderson intended. All he had to do was leave her, and the winter weather would do the rest. By morning she would be dead. She would not see Leo again; not be able to tell him she still loved him; never feel his arms around her, holding her close to his heart. Scalding tears trickled down her cheeks and she cursed her kidnappers, shouting out a stream of invectives she had learnt from listening to Leo.

★ ★ ★

Mary could see little through the tiny panes of the attic window. She decided to open it, no one would see her, so high up. Cautiously she peeped through the gap. The soldiers were grouped in formation, guns pointing towards the screaming mob. There appeared to be about thirty ill-dressed men, rattling the gate. Occasional missiles hurtled over the top to land harmlessly in the grass in front of the armed men.

Satisfied they were in no immediate danger Mary closed the window and latched it carefully. The sun was low and the light beginning to fade. Full darkness could not be more than an hour or so away. Surely the men outside would give up then and return to their homes, or move to an easier target?

Halfway down the winding attic stairs, Mary began to feel dizzy and was forced to lean heavily against the wall for support. Miss Ellie had been right; she had got up too soon. She feared she would be unable to reach her room before she fainted. By the time she had groped her way to her bed her head was pounding and blackness threatened to engulf her. She would just have a little rest; she felt sure her mistress would forgive her lapse when she realized how unwell she was.

She had intended to close her eyes for a few minutes, just lie down and allow the faintness and nausea to pass. She had got up too soon and her exertions had proved too much. She fell into a deep sleep as soon as her head touched the pillow.

The sun set and the bitter east wind, which had travelled straight from Russia, began to sober the mob outside the gates. First singly, then in groups of two or three, they slunk away, fading into the darkness. They had not expected the manor to be so well protected; but they would regroup and return. There were rich pickings to be had at Wenham, so they had been told, more than enough food to keep all of them, and their families, for the rest of the winter.

John watched the last of them vanish. 'Is that it, Jenkins? Are we safe?'

Jenkins stamped his frozen feet, hoping to restore some circulation. 'No, I'm afraid not, sir. Tomorrow, they will be more determined to get in. Couldn't you hear what they were shouting as they left?' John shook his head; he had been positioned too far away to hear. 'They said they will come tomorrow and bring more men. News of this will have spread and malcontents, from other villages and towns, will flood to join them.'

'What about the militia? Can we send someone to raise them?'

'I have done so. I sent a message to Sir John Russell, your nearest influential neighbour, telling him what is happening here. It is up to him now.'

John frowned. 'His estate is a good twenty miles from here. I hope he thinks the threat is sufficient to warrant action on his part. One thing I've learnt these past few weeks is that folks round here look after their own, but aren't so willing to take risks for their neighbours.'

Jenkins shrugged. 'Well, sir, there's naught we can do about it now. The colonel will be here soon and, with him in command, there will be no need for the militia.' He called to his men. 'Stand easy, men. There'll be no further trouble tonight.' He pointed. 'You two, take first watch. I'll have some hot food and a couple of lanterns sent out to you.'

His men, well satisfied with their day's work, plodded after Jenkins back to the stables, where they were billeted. One of the rooms above the stalls was their temporary home. It was warm and cosy and their straw beds were vermin free. The lights had not been lit in the downstairs rooms of the manor and John felt a moment of anxiety. Why was Lady Upminster in the dark? Where was everyone? He increased his pace and was running by the time he reached the back door. It was locked, as it should be. He pounded on the door, demanding to be let in.

Hurrying footsteps and rattles indicated someone was at the door. The light flooded the path. Jenny, one of the parlour maids, smiled a welcome.

'Where is Lady Upminster? Why is the house in darkness?'

'I don't rightly know, sir; we have been in the kitchen this past two hours preparing food for all the extra men. Cook has a tasty stew — '

'Damn the stew, girl. Where is your mistress? Where is Smith? Get the candles and lamps lit immediately.'

'Yes, sir, at once. Shall I fetch Smith here, first?'

'No, I will find her myself.' John strode down the corridor carrying his flickering candlelight aloft. He banged on Smith's private parlour door. He heard sounds of movement and slow footsteps before the door opened.

'Mr Jones, come in. I'm sorry I must have dozed off.' John swallowed his pithy reply. Smith was over seventy; it was hardly surprising she fell asleep in front of her fire sometimes.

'Where are Lady Upminster and Mary, Smith? The house is in darkness. It would not be seemly for me to search upstairs; I need you to organize this at once.'

Smith pushed her grey hair back under her cap and straightened her clothes. 'I will go myself, Mr Jones. Wait in the hall. I will not be long.'

John walked impatiently up and down the flagged hall, grateful for the steady warmth coming from the huge fireplace. This fire was never allowed to go out. He heard voices upstairs. Smith had found someone, but was it his Mary or Miss Ellie?

Mary appeared first, leaning heavily on the banister. 'Oh dear, John. She is not up here. Her room is empty, but her thick cloak and boots are gone.'

It was as he feared. He watched as Mary swayed dangerously halfway up the stairs. 'Mary, love, you should not be up. There is nothing you can do. Smith, please take Mary back to her room and attend to her. I will rouse the men to search for Lady Upminster.'

It was dark and flakes of snow were falling,

blown in swirling clouds by the east wind. John locked the side door and returned to the kitchen. 'Lady Upminster is missing. I'm going down to the stables to get Jenkins to organize the search.' Fear for his young mistress soured his belly. She had not been seen for hours; she could be anywhere by now.

As he left by the back door he heard the sound of shouting coming from the front gate and halted. The men left on guard were challenging someone. Then he heard the gate being opened and three caped and muffled riders galloped out of the blizzard.

'My Lord Upminster; thank God you are here.' John called, as he watched the men sway tiredly from their saddles.

This greeting sent a shock of apprehension down Leo's spine. He threw his reins to Jess and strode across. 'What is wrong?'

'Lady Upminster is missing.'

'For God's sake, what do you mean, missing? Have you searched the house and grounds?'

'Only the house, so far, my lord. Her disappearance was not discovered until I returned fifteen minutes ago. I'm on the way to the stable to organize the men.'

Leo stared hard at John; he saw a middle-aged man, tired beyond endurance.

'Go back to the kitchen and rest, get something to eat. Your job is done.' He turned and ran towards the stables where Jenkins, alerted by his voice, was turning out the men. 'Jenkins, Lady Upminster has been taken. Search the stables and close vicinity for evidence.' Leo knew it would be a futile exercise to search the grounds. His wife had been kidnapped; he was certain of it. What he was equally certain was that the perpetrators were living on borrowed time.

'Sam, take some men and go into the village; find out what you can about this man Anderson. Discover who is in his employ and then bring me two of them; I will question them myself.'

Sam selected a handful of men and, freshly mounted, rode off towards the village. He checked his pistol was to hand and his sabre loose within its scabbard. They would be needed tonight. 'Jenkins, have your men eaten today?'

'No, my lord, not yet.'

'Send them to the kitchen. They will be no use to me half dead with fatigue and hunger.' Jenkins shouted out his orders and the remaining men trooped off happily. A hot meal in a warm room would restore their morale as much as their bodies.

'Jenkins, come with me; we can talk whilst I

change and get something to eat.' Leo, his saddle-bags slung over his shoulder, met Smith on his way upstairs. 'Smith, have hot water and whatever the men are eating, sent upstairs.' He paused and frowned. 'Which is my room, Smith? You had better show me.'

The elderly housekeeper retraced her steps and took him to the master suite. 'These are Lady Upminster's rooms, my lord, the room next door is the Master's chamber.'

'Excellent. Now have that food and water sent immediately. I wish to be ready to ride out again in thirty minutes.'

'I'm afraid the fire's not lit in the main chamber, my lord. I will see to it immediately but Lady Upminster's room is always warm.'

'I will use Lady Upminster's room but have the other prepared for me. I will need it later, no doubt.'

Smith scuttled off and Leo, with Jenkins at his heels, stepped into his wife's bedchamber. The room where Eleanor had slept alone, away from him, for the past few weeks. The room was dominated by an enormous, old-fashioned, heavy oak bedstead. His eyes narrowed and his nostrils flared at the images that flooded his mind.

Angrily he shook his head. He had decided to give Ellie her freedom, if she wanted it; so such fantasies were pointless. He flung his bags on the floor dropped on to the fireside chair wondering if dry clothes were really worth the trouble of taking off his boots.

'Allow me, sir.' Jenkins deftly removed both boots and set them down beside the fire to gently steam. Leo slumped back, closing his eyes for a few moments, trying to marshal his thoughts. This was one campaign he could not afford to lose; if he got this wrong it was the life of his precious wife that could be snuffed out.

24

Voices were approaching the hut and Eleanor knew, instinctively, that this was not the sound of a rescue party she could hear. It was her captors returning, expecting her to be cowed and shivering with fear. She was an Upminster; she would not succumb so easily. If she was to die tonight, it would be sitting up, facing her murderers, defiantly.

Pride and anger gave her strength to roll over on to her front, then caterpillar-like she inched and wriggled until she felt the wall against her back. The voices were nearer; she was not going to have time to complete the task.

Desperately she drew her bound knees up towards her face and stretched her fingers down until they could grasp the ropes that restricted her legs. Then as the bar was being lifted from the door she braced her back, shuffled her bottom and she was sitting upright, facing the opening door. She realized she was feeling considerably warmer; her effort had restored some warmth to her frozen limbs.

A lantern was held high, temporarily

blinding her; she blinked rapidly, wanting to see who her captors were. The black shapes at the door moved forward and she instantly recognized one of them. It was, as she had suspected, the hated Anderson, come to gloat at her misfortune.

'Well, well, not so high and mighty now, are we, my lady?' Anderson sneered.

'I do not see what you hope to gain by this abduction. If I do not return to Wenham, Lord Upminster will hunt you down and kill you.'

'Lord Upminster will be glad I have rid him of an unwanted burden. Why else would he banish you to this backwater?'

'You are mistaken; he is, at this very moment, riding here. There is still time for you to save your life; release me and you might still live.'

Anderson stared down at the dilapidated bundle glaring so defiantly back at him. His thin lips curved in the semblance of a smile. 'If what you say is true, then my days are numbered anyway. If you're lying then your demise can only be of benefit to me.'

'My people will know it was you. Are you so stupid you have not realized yet, that your tenure as estate manager was over as soon as an Upminster took up residence at Wenham?' She had his full attention now.

'Whilst Lord Upminster did not know this estate existed you were safe. Whatever happens to me he will retain all that is his; including your house and certainly your life. The rich remain so because they never let the money owed to them go unrepaid.'

The two unkempt men, who had accompanied Anderson, began to mutter to themselves. They knew what she said was true. Whatever the outcome of tonight's events, their master's days of power were over and their own lives in mortal danger.

Eleanor watched them sidle backwards and disappear into the blackness. Anderson hesitated, then he turned to leave also. 'Mr Anderson, please untie me; I can find my own way home. Surely you do not wish to have my death on your conscience?'

He stopped and his empty eyes met hers. 'It don't matter to me, either way. In fact it will please me to know you have perished, for your interference has ruined my life.'

The door closed plunging her back into freezing darkness and Eleanor's defiance crumpled. She had failed. She was going to be left to die in a miserable hovel and there was nothing she could do about it, apart from pray.

She stiffened, alerted by the sound of stealthy footsteps approaching her prison again. Anderson, or one of his henchmen, had changed his mind and was returning to silence her, for ever.

★ ★ ★

Leo was back downstairs, changed, fed and much restored, as two of Jenkins's men appeared at the kitchen door. 'Anything?'

'Yes, my lord. There are signs of a struggle in the empty stall at the end of the row. It was hard to search outside, what with the snow and the dark but there is a trail of broken branches leading away towards the village.'

'Good man. You have confirmed what I already suspected. Send Sam to me if he returns before we leave; now get something to eat and drink. I will need you again soon.'

Leo turned to Jenkins. 'How well do you know this area, Jenkins?'

'Well enough, my lord. What do you wish to know?'

'Is there a hostelry in the village? Somewhere the malcontents can meet and gain courage from their ale?'

'Indeed there is, my lord, at Wenham village. It is a rat hole, little better than the hovels they live in.'

Leo looked at his fob watch. 'The ringleaders will be nursing their grievances over an ale pot. I want all the men, armed and ready, outside in ten minutes. We are going to Wenham; I dare not wait for Sam to return. We must hope we meet him on the way.'

If the men thought a march through the snow, in the dark, was asking too much of them, they didn't say so. They were battle-hardened soldiers and went where they were bid, without complaint. Having a full belly made them ready for anything.

John wanted to join them but was told to stay and guard the manor. If Lord Upminster did not think him up to the task ahead he knew better than to argue. The grim-faced stranger commanding the expedition was not a man to quarrel with.

'Jenkins, I want the men marching in file; heavy footed, fully armed; let the rabble know we are coming to rout them.'

'Yes, my lord.' Jenkins returned to his troops smiling silently. His old commander had lost none of his skill. When the men, half sozzled, heard marching feet outside, they would think the militia had arrived. The rest would be easy.

Lanterns swaying, blobs of brightness in the white, the men set out, Leo riding behind, mounted on a sturdy hunter. He forced himself to concentrate on the task in hand when his every sinew screamed to be searching and rescuing his beloved Ellie. He knew, what a lesser man might not, unless he disbanded the mob first, not just his wife would die, but dozens of women and children. The militia would be mustering in Norwich and when they descended on an area death and destruction followed in full measure.

Sam's small group met Leo as they reached the outskirts of the village. 'My lord, I have two of the ringleaders here. Do you wish to speak to them?'

'Bring them. Let us get this over with.' Leo dismounted smoothly and gestured for his men to form a circle of light around him. Sam dragged the terrified men forwards; they had been forced to run behind the horses, roped together by the hands. Whatever defiance the men might have been considering crumbled when they saw the formidable giant waiting to question them. They saw a bloody death staring them in the face.

'You will tell me now, who is behind this trouble?' Leo did not need to ask a second time. In moments he had all the information he needed to hang Anderson and his henchmen. 'Sam, you and Davies come with me. Jenkins, take these objects back to the village. They can tell the rest of the

292

miscreants what will happen if they are still there when I arrive tomorrow morning.'

Leo watched Jenkins lead the prisoners back along the lane, satisfied the danger from civil unrest was over. Now he could concentrate on finding Eleanor and punishing her attackers.

'We need to travel quietly, Sam. Anderson will have guards on the door; we do not want to alert them.'

The snow underfoot cushioned their progress and apart from the occasional jangle of a bit the four men travelled silently in the silvery light. Leo reined in. The others halted behind him. He had heard voices coming from the lane ahead.

Silently, he dismounted and, with his hand over the nostrils of his mount, led it up the bank and into the field above. He was followed by one other horseman. Sam vanished, in similar fashion, up the bank on the far side of the path.

Leo drew his sabre and crouched, coiled to spring upon the men approaching in the lane below. These were the animals who had abducted Eleanor. His mind was clear: his decision made. The two men walked blindly into his trap. It was over in seconds. They fell dead in their tracks, snuffed out instantly, given no time to cry a warning to anyone else waiting by the hut.

Leo wiped his sabre blade casually on his breeches and slid it back into its scabbard. Two men had died and not a word had been spoken. Leaving the horses on the bank he gestured towards the silhouette and they crept forward, almost invisible against the hedgerow. Sam took a man and circled left, Leo with the other, went right. There was no sign of anyone else on guard, but Leo never took chances.

He raised his fist; Sam and the men understood and all dropped to one knee in the snow, rifles cocked and raised, ready to fire if anyone appeared in the doorway.

Leo reached the door and carefully lifted the bar. He stood to one side, pistol out, and yanked the door open, ready to fire. He paused, holding his breath, waiting; then he heard a sound from within. He dropped his pistol and charged, caution forgotten, into the hovel. Eleanor was alive!

'Leo, oh Leo, thank God, it is you! I thought it was Anderson returning to finish me.'

'Ellie, sweetheart, what has he done to you? Sit still, I will have these undone in a second.' Eleanor heard him slice through the ropes with a knife he had pulled with the ease of long practice, from inside his boot. A lantern was lit, and held up, by one of his men.

Suddenly her arms and legs were free, but for some reason they refused to move. She had been held for so long in one position all feeling had vanished. As though from a distance she watched Leo remove his coat and place it around her shoulders. The warmth and familiar smell added to the unreality. Was this a dream, was she imagining her rescue?

Then she felt herself being lifted into the safety of his arms. 'Ellie, Ellie, talk to me. Are you hurt? Darling, did he harm you?' Leo's urgent question and vigorous shake forced her to concentrate. She was so cold she was finding it difficult to speak. She leant closer, resting her dirty face on his chest. 'I am well, now you are here, Leo, but so cold . . . so very cold.' Her voice was little more than a whisper, but enough to reassure him.

'I will have you safe and warm very soon, my love. And no one will ever harm you again; I will take better care of you in future.'

Leo regained his feet and, holding his precious burden to his heart, he stepped out into the moonlight. His broad back made a perfect target. Sam, a fraction too late, had seen Leo's assailant. Anderson did not live to see the havoc his shot had caused.

Leo staggered and fell to his knees, still

cradling Eleanor. 'Sam, take her,' he groaned, but managed to stay upright just long enough for Sam to drop his smoking rifle and leap forward to catch the unconscious girl. Leo, his mission complete, pitched into the snow, and joined his wife in the twilight world that hovered between life and death.

★　★　★

It was the smell of hot toast and melted butter that finally roused Eleanor from her stupor. She rolled over, yawned, stretched and blinked opened her eyes. Then she blinked again, not sure her first glance had been correct.

'Yes, child, it is I, Sophia, come to minister to the invalids.'

Eleanor pushed herself up on to her elbows and stared open-mouthed at her fashion-conscious sister-in-law dressed in a brown dress, with high collar and long, neatly buttoned sleeves. She was not sure if the plain outfit, or Sophia's presence in her bedchamber, surprised her most.

'What are you doing here? I do not understand at all.'

Sophia grinned, an expression seen as rarely as a plain outfit. 'It is a long story.' She placed the tray of hot toast and weak tea down on the side table within easy reach of her patient. 'Here, let me help to sit you up. I expect you are as weak as a kitten.' She grasped Eleanor firmly under the arms and expertly moved her up the bed. She had obviously done this before, another surprise! 'Do you know, you have been asleep for three days? I woke you sometimes and spooned water down your throat, but you haven't fully revived, until now.'

'There is something else I have not done for three days, Sophia. I must get up, now, at once.' Her urgent tone carried a hint of desperation. Sophia deftly flicked back the covers and helped Eleanor swing her legs to the floor.

'Let me help you, my dear; your legs will be wobbly after so long in bed.' The trip to the discreetly screened commode and back taxed Eleanor's depleted strength and she was glad to regain the comfort of her bed. Her stomach gurgled alarmingly startling both women into fits of giggles.

Sophia put the tray across Eleanor's lap. 'Here, I think this is what you need.' The toast was rapidly demolished and the tea drunk thirstily.

Eleanor leant back feeling almost like her old self. 'Now, Sophia, tell me how you come to be at Wenham, acting nursemaid to me.'

Her sister-in-law pulled up a stool and sat down. 'When you ran away, the duke was beside himself. It is odd, but after so many years without seeing, or speaking of his youngest son, now he can think, and converse, of nothing else.'

'I suppose, having rejected Leo so unkindly, he is afraid he will die before he has made amends.'

Sophia nodded. 'Yes, I am sure that is correct. Anyway, when the message came to say you had been found, the duke decided we must up sticks and travel at once to Monk's Hall, to be there to welcome you back.'

'He was very sure Leo would persuade me, then?'

'All the Upminsters get their own way in the end, do you not realize that?'

Eleanor smiled. 'Of course, I do. Now, go on; you are all at Monk's Hall, I follow the tale so far, but how are you now at Wenham?'

'His grace was not satisfied with waiting, he decided we should travel on, regardless of either our, or your, feelings, on the subject. Gareth tried to explain you would need time alone together to sort out your differences, but the duke, as usual, ignored him. He insisted that Leo would need his trappings, as he left with only a single change of raiment in his saddle-bags. And so, here we are.'

She looked round the sparsely furnished room. 'While I am glad I came, no one else could have acted as nurse, I will be relieved when you are both well enough to travel back to the comfort of Monk's Hall.'

Eleanor sat upright, her complexion pale. 'Both? Sophia, is Leo hurt? I must go to him.' Sophia mentally cursed her slip; it had been their intention to allow Eleanor to recover fully before she learnt of her husband's injury. 'Leo is going to make a full recovery, my dear. Gareth and the duke are watching over him like hens over a single chick.' She smiled, glad to see some pink returning to Eleanor's cheeks. 'Poor Sam is hardly allowed to help at all.'

'Poor Leo, you mean.' Eleanor relaxed again, her initial panic over. 'He must hate all the fussing. He will recover far better if affairs are left to his man.'

Eleanor leant out of the bed, almost losing her balance, and grabbed the bell strap, giving it a vigorous pull. 'In fact, I am going to insist that Sam is put in charge.' Sophia opened her mouth to protest but changed her mind. Mary came in, bobbing a curtsy to the marchioness, before turning, face wreathed in smiles, to Eleanor.

'You are awake at last, my lady, we have been that worried. What can I get for you?'

'I wish you to relieve the marchioness from her duties as my maid. And I wish Sam to resume his duties with Lord Upminster immediately.'

'I will do so at once, my lady.' She paused, a possible problem occurring to all of them. 'When I speak to Sam, or . . . ?'

Sophia laughed. 'No, Mary, you can leave it to me. I will go at once to Lord Upminster's chamber and deliver Lady Upminster's message.'

Eleanor's plan had worked, as she knew it would. When the door closed behind Sophia she turned to Mary. 'I need a hot bath, Mary. I still have the smell of the hovel on my hair. After that I wish to get up.'

'There is a bath being sent up already, my lady. You relax a while; you have had a nasty experience.'

'It appears it was not as nasty as Lord Upminster's. How was he injured?'

Mary hesitated, not sure if it was her place to tell her mistress the details. 'He was shot in the back, by that devil Anderson, but it was a clean wound and he is making a full recovery.'

'And Anderson?'

'Dead, my lady; Sam shot him.'

'Good. I am glad; he was a wicked man.'

Mary busied herself placing screens and

setting up a hip bath in front of the fire. Then she hung several towels to warm on a wooden stand. The sound of shuffling footsteps heralded the arrival of hot water.

Eleanor hated that it involved so much backbreaking work for so many people whenever she wanted to bathe. When they returned to Monk's Hall she would insist Leo put in water closets and fixed baths in the dressing-rooms attached to the main suites. At least then only the hot water would have to be carried upstairs, for the cold would exit through the pipes attached to the bath.

It was only then she realized she had forgiven Leo, and was prepared to start again. At the thought of what this would mean her blood surged round her body. There was so much she still had to learn about Leo, and more importantly, about being a wife. She couldn't wait for the instruction to begin.

The warm bath restored her and removed the final residue of her captivity from her person. She sat, cross-legged, in front of the roaring fire whilst Mary brushed her hair dry. 'It will have to do, Mary; I wish to get dressed. Find something pretty for me; I do not care what, but please make sure it has long sleeves and a warm underskirt.' She had Mary arrange her freshly washed hair simply behind her head then thread it with a ribbon, leaving it hanging down in a heavy dark cloud.

The dress she wore was, as were most of her clothes, too loose, but the high waist and wide hem helped to disguise her loss of weight. The russet colour suited her, making her eyes appear more tawny than green. 'Are you finished, Mary? The sash is tied beautifully and my wrap is arranged just as it should be. Please stop fussing and let me go.'

Mary knew, even if her mistress did not, that, for this first meeting with Lord Upminster, after so many weeks apart, Lady Upminster should look her best. 'There, I am done. You look lovely, my lady. A little darkness under the eyes is all there is to show of your ordeal.'

'Thank you, Mary.' She walked towards the communicating door, desperate to see Leo, but suddenly reluctant to go in. As she hesitated, Mary took matters into her own hands and knocked hard on the door.

25

The room was empty of unwanted helpers who had taken the hint and gone. The four-poster bed made even Leo appear small. At the sound of the communicating door opening, he turned his head tiredly. Then his mouth curved into a smile of joy and his eyes glittered with an emotion he quickly disguised.

'Ellie, my dear, come in. I have been worried about you.'

She glided towards the still figure in the bed. To her dismay, it appeared that Sophia had been untruthful. Leo was far from well. His face had an unhealthy pallor and he hardly had the strength to raise his head. 'I am afraid that I cannot say the same, Leo.' His expression of surprise at her blunt statement made her smile. 'I meant, I was unaware you had been hurt until an hour ago. You do not look at all recovered.'

Leo patted the tapestry-seated chair, placed conveniently beside the bed. 'Thank you, Eleanor; it is good to know I am doing so well.'

'Idiot! I meant Sophia told me you are

almost better, but I can see that is not the case at all.' She smiled, no trace of animosity in her expression. 'If you have had both the duke and Gareth in here fussing, it is hardly surprising you are not making progress. I have had them sent away; Sam and I can take care of you now.'

'There is no need for you to concern yourself, my dear. Sam can manage on his own. You have also been unwell and must not overtax yourself on my behalf.'

Eleanor sensed a certain reservation in his tone. Did he not want her help? She sat back, thinking rapidly. Was he too sick to discuss the issues that had separated them? 'Leo, we need to talk. I know you are unwell, but I have things I must say to you and I cannot leave them unsaid any longer.'

'You are quite right. There are also things I must say to you.' He smiled sadly, knowing what he had to do, but dreading the pain it would cause him. 'Shall I speak first? After all I am, as you so kindly reminded me, 'not looking at all recovered'.'

Eleanor braced herself to suffer what was obviously going to be unpleasant news. 'Very well, my lord, what is it you wish to say to me?' She sat back, her expression polite, her eyes guarded.

'Ellie, this is hard for me to say. In fact, the

words are choking me, but say them I will.' He swallowed twice. 'I wish to annul the marriage; to give you your freedom. The duke has given me the estates that my mother left me, and my title is no longer one of courtesy only.' He steeled himself to glance across expecting to see relief and happiness on his wife's face. He saw tears trickling down her ashen cheeks. 'I thought you would be pleased. I am giving you Monk's Hall and the funds Aunt Prudence left. You are an independent woman now. Is that not what you always wanted?'

She struggled to reply, her throat was so thick with tears. 'No, of course it is not. I love you, Leo. I want to be your wife; I want to have your children; share Monk's Hall with you; not grow old and lonely there, on my own.'

Leo stared at her, stunned by her revelation. Then, to her astonishment, he stretched out a suspiciously strong arm and tumbled her on to the bed. 'My darling girl; I cannot believe you love me after all I have done to you. I have loved you since I first set eyes on you, as a gawky schoolgirl of fourteen years.' He grinned at her look of disbelief. 'It is true, my love, it is just that I did not recognize the fact until I thought you had gone for ever.'

Eleanor wriggled upright her face suffused with happiness.

'And I have loved you since that time, but I discovered the fact a little sooner.'

He reached out and, with his thumb, rubbed away her tears. 'Tell me, when did you realize that you loved me?'

'It was when I thought Rufus had killed you. I thought I was going to lose you and I knew that without you my life would be meaningless.'

He took a hand and pulled her down to nestle contentedly against his sound shoulder. He settled his arm about her waist and, with a smile of total contentment on his face, he fell asleep, trapping Eleanor beside him. She raised her head and drank in his beloved features, noticing with a pang how thin his face had become, how deep the lines either side of his mouth.

But he was no longer the pale, drawn man she had seen on her entrance; his face was now a healthy pink and his mouth relaxed, even in sleep, into a happy smile. Satisfied, she laid her head back gently and closed her eyes, allowing her breathing to slowly attune to his.

★　★　★

His Grace, the Duke of Rothmere, stood outside the bedchamber door as determined to gain admittance as Sam was to keep him out. 'Stand aside, man, I wish to speak to my son.'

'I am sorry, your grace, his lordship is resting and must not be disturbed.'

'I will be the judge of that. Get out of my way, I say. I will not be argued with.' The raised voice brought both Sophia and Gareth hurrying down the corridor.

'Your grace,' Gareth remonstrated gently, 'come away. Eleanor is with Leo; did you not know that?'

'Good God!' The duke beamed at Sam. 'Good man! Well done, well done indeed.' He turned, still smiling. 'Leo will get well now; all the boy needed was his wife beside him.' He chuckled. 'I never thought to see a soldier so reduced by love.'

Sam remained on guard outside the door while Lord and Lady Upminster slept entwined in each other's arms. It was Leo who woke first. 'My darling, I am afraid you will have to move.'

Sleepily she yawned, then, fully awake, realized the problem. 'I am so sorry, Leo, I must have fallen asleep.'

He grinned and gingerly flexed his arm, trying to restore some life to it. 'Do not apologize, sweetheart, that was the first real rest I have had for several weeks. A stiff arm is a small price to pay.'

Eleanor shifted across the covers and regained her feet. 'It is getting dark, Leo. We must have been asleep for hours.' She pulled the bell strap. 'We need the lamps lit and the fire is almost out.'

A knock on the door startled both of them. 'Come,' Leo called.

Sam stepped in, a sheepish grin on his face. 'I heard you stirring, my lord, lady. Shall I light the lamps and rekindle the fire?'

'Have you been outside the door, all this time, Sam?'

His man nodded. 'You needed some peace, my lord. You have had precious little of it these last few days.'

Leo ran his hand over the dark stubble on his chin. 'I think hot water is called for. Ellie, my love, leave me now in Sam's capable hands. Do not go far; as soon as I am respectable I wish you to return.'

'I think you look like a brigand, Leo. I rather like it, it complements your personality.'

'Impertinent chit! Have you no respect?'

'None at all. How long will he be, Sam?'

'Give us an hour, my lady. Shall I send for you?'

308

She nodded. 'Yes, please. I will be downstairs somewhere, I expect.' She left the room, leaving Leo still chuckling.

Mary was waiting anxiously for her mistress. 'There you are, my lady. Good heavens, that dress looks as though you have been asleep in it.'

'I have, Mary. Do I need to change, or can you repair the damage?'

Mary surveyed the crumpled gown and shook her head. 'It will not do, I'm afraid. It is almost time to change for dinner anyway. I will get out a suitable gown.' Eleanor looked mutinous. 'You have guests, my lady. They will expect you to dress.'

'Oh, very well. I did not wish to eat downstairs. I intended to share a tray with Lord Upminster. We have so much catching up to do.'

'My lady, the duke and the marquis and marchioness have dined alone for three nights; it would not be right to ignore them now you are well.'

Eleanor submitted to Mary's ministrations and an hour later she was resplendent in her peach silk dinner gown, with her hair swept up into a knot on top of her head. She stared at her reflection. 'It is a shame I had to sell my amber beads. They went so well with this dress.'

There was a soft tap on the communicating door. 'It will be Sam, telling me I can go in.' She heard the door open.

'I rather thought you would need these this evening, my love.' Her eyes flew up to meet Leo's in the mirror. He was dressed formally in his evening black, the empty sleeve, on the right, the only indication of his injury. He stepped close and placed an open jewel box on the dressing-table. It was her amber necklace.

'I do not understand; I sold these in Norwich a few days ago.'

He smiled. 'And I bought these in Norwich a few days ago. Do not look so surprised, darling girl; I knew you would have to sell your jewellery and Jenkins had the funds to purchase them.' He ran his hand over the golden stones. 'They are lovely, but not good enough for you. We will go to town, and purchase you something more suitable.'

'Town?' Eleanor replied faintly. 'In season?'

He grinned, delighted at her stunned reaction. 'I am a reformed character; I intend to take you to every ball and soirée of importance. I will even dance a cotillion with you.'

She spun, her dress a blur of colour, and placed a hand on her husband's arm. 'It is very kind of you to offer, Leo, but I would

310

much prefer to stay at home with you.'

He clasped her small hand in his and raised it to his lips. Smiling down at her he kissed first the tips of her fingers, then turned it and pressed his mouth to her palm. He raised his head, his eyes dark with love. 'I rather hoped you would say that, my love, but I felt I had to offer.'

Impulsively she stretched up and placed a feather-light kiss on his mouth, intending her gesture to merely indicate her pleasure. To Leo it meant something else entirely. He released her hand and placed his one arm around her waist to bring her hard against him. His mouth sought hers and she tipped her head to receive his kiss.

A slight sound from Mary, standing behind them, caused Leo to raise his head. 'I am afraid, my darling, that duty calls.' He dropped his arm, moved back a step, and lifted the amber beads from their box. 'Shall I fasten these, for you, sweetheart?'

She grinned. 'With one hand? That would be impressive!'

'We shall do it together. If you stand still, I will hold them whilst you do up the clasp.'

They both knew it would have been more sensible to hand the necklace to Mary, but they wanted to prolong the moment of intimacy.

'There, my love, you look ravishing.' Leo looked closer and frowned. 'But you are far too thin. You have not been looking after yourself properly. All that will change now I am here to take care of you.'

'I am not the only one who has lost weight. You are a shadow of your former self, my love.'

Leo grinned and pulled Eleanor's arm through his. 'Obviously we cannot manage without each other. A matter that has now, I sincerely hope, been permanently remedied.'

They heard the dinner gong and the sound of voices passing the closed door. 'We must go down, Ellie. It is the least we can do after the duke and Gareth and Sophia, have driven all this way to see us.'

Eleanor suddenly became aware that Leo was leaning on her, not the other way round. She glanced anxiously at his face, noting the tense lines around his mouth. 'You are not well, Leo. This is ridiculous. You should be in your bed.'

'I am fine, my dear, please do not fuss. We are going down to dinner, not for a five-mile route march.'

Eleanor remained stationary. 'We will only go down, Leo, if you promise me you will return to your room as soon as the meal is over.'

'Very well; now, shall we go?'

Three heads swivelled to greet them as they entered the dining-room. All three drew breath to suggest Leo had come down too soon but on seeing his scowl, wisely kept quiet.

The duke moved over to his son. 'Come and sit down, my boy; we are all delighted to see you up and about again.'

Leo allowed himself to be led towards the table, a pale smile fixed his lips. 'Thank you, your grace. We did not wish you to eat alone for a fourth night, did we, my dear?'

Ellie had already been seated but didn't reply until Leo was safely installed in his chair as well. 'No, we did not. But I am afraid I am still feeling a little weak, so hope you will excuse me if I retire early, your grace?' Murmurs of assent rippled round the table. Leo flashed her a grateful glance, knowing her departure would allow him to leave early also.

During the second remove of jugged hare, quails in honey, assorted buttered vegetables and cream vanilla jellies, the duke turned to his youngest son.

'Well, Leo, my boy, what you going to do with Wenham Manor, now? You and Eleanor are not intending to live here, are you?'

'Good grief! I hope not!' Leo looked at his

wife. 'Do you want to return to Monk's Hall, Ellie?'

'Yes, of course I do, it is my home.' She blushed and corrected herself. 'It is our home.'

The duke beamed. 'Excellent, excellent: it is too far to travel for a visit to this benighted neck of the woods.'

Leo sat back, his colour much restored after consuming a hearty meal. 'I had thought, Ellie my dear, that maybe John Jones would like to become our estate manager here? He seems to have been doing an efficient job so far.' Eleanor's smile of delight at the suggestion made verbal agreement unnecessary. 'In that case, I will speak to him tomorrow.'

Impulsively, she leant across the table and clasped his hand. 'Thank you, Leo; it is a wonderful gesture. I know John wishes to marry Mary and now he can do so. I will miss her; she has been a friend as well as an employee these past five years, but she deserves to be as happy as I am and so does John.'

It was as though they were alone in the room. Leo's eyes glowed and his hand tightened over hers. 'I love you, Ellie, and intend to spend the rest of my life making you happy.'

'Eerrr . . . umm . . . ' the duke cleared his throat politely, not wishing his besotted son to embarrass himself further. Leo didn't release her hand at first, but when he felt her trying to pull away he immediately let go. He sat back with a contented smile and spoke directly to Gareth.

'It is going to be some time before matters are sorted out here, Gareth. There is Anderson's house to sell, and I will have to engage lawyers to draw up an agreement for Jones to sign. These things cannot be accomplished overnight.'

Gareth took the hint. 'And we have to return to Rothmere. We have been away from the children too long already, have we not, Sophia my dear?'

For an instant Sophia looked blank. The three boys were well cared for by a team of nannies, and tutors, and would scarcely have noticed their fond parents' departure. Gareth raised an eyebrow in the duke's direction.

'Indeed we have, my love. Now that our patients are almost well again we will not linger.' She smiled at her father-in-law. 'Your grace, can you be ready to depart tomorrow morning?'

'Depart? So soon?' The duke was not a stupid man, but knew he had been outmanoeuvred. 'Yes, of course I can, my

315

dear Sophia. We will depart as soon as we have broken our fast.'

Leo, having achieved his objective, nodded to his father. 'If you will excuse me, your grace, it has been a long evening and I am beginning to flag.'

Eleanor took her cue. 'As I am, your grace. It has been a delightful evening and when we are re-established at Monk's Hall I hope you will all come and visit?' She smiled mischievously at Sophia. 'Please bring the boys, Sophia, I can understand how you hate to be apart from them.'

Sophia's look of horror at the helpful suggestion was almost Eleanor's undoing. Somehow she managed to hide her amusement as a footman pulled out her chair.

The marchioness recovered quickly. 'Thank you so much for the kind invitation, my dear Eleanor. Gareth and I will be delighted to visit when the weather improves.'

The duke, and Gareth, rose politely. Eleanor took Leo's arm and felt it quivering beneath her touch. She dared not look up and catch his eye. Leo bid his family a choked goodnight and they hurried from the room. They managed to reach the stairs before they dissolved into laughter.

Leo leaned against the wall, tears of mirth trickling down his face. 'Oh God, Ellie, you are incorrigible!' he spluttered. 'Laughing so much has set my shoulder off again.'

Instantly she sobered. 'Leo, I am so sorry. Let me help you upstairs. I will call Sam to take care of you.'

He pushed himself away from the wall, his expression tender. 'It is not Sam, I wish to take care of me tonight, my darling, it is you.' He traced the outline of her parted lips with his forefinger and her knees trembled. 'Are you ready, little bird? I have waited a lifetime for this moment, and if you are sure, I do not wish to wait another minute.' His hot eyes consumed her with passion and she almost fell into his embrace.

Leo braced himself against the wall and lifted his wife from her feet, holding her captive; her softness moulded to his hard contours; he plundered her waiting mouth in a kiss that told Eleanor all she needed to know about his feelings.

A long time later he relaxed his hold and lowered her gently to her feet. 'This is not the place for this, my love. Will you come with me and let me show you how much I love you?'

Eleanor placed her hand on his empty sleeve. 'Are you sure you are well enough? You have just spent three days in your bed.'

'And that is where I hope to spend the next three days, my darling, but this time I do not wish to be alone. Will you join me, Ellie, my love?'

Speechless with joy she placed her hand trustingly in his. Together, at last, they headed for the bedroom to share their love in the way that all lovers do.

★ ★ ★

Downstairs, in the dining-room, His Grace, the Duke of Rothmere, stood, and raised his brimming glass, a rare smile softening his austere features. 'Let us toast my youngest son and his beautiful wife. May they be as happy for the rest of their lives, as they are this night.'

We do hope that you have enjoyed reading this large print book.

Did you know that all of our titles are available for purchase?

We publish a wide range of high quality large print books including:
Romances, Mysteries, Classics
General Fiction
Non Fiction and Westerns

Special interest titles available in large print are:
The Little Oxford Dictionary
Music Book
Song Book
Hymn Book
Service Book

Also available from us courtesy of Oxford University Press:
Young Readers' Dictionary
(large print edition)
Young Readers' Thesaurus
(large print edition)

For further information or a free brochure, please contact us at:
Ulverscroft Large Print Books Ltd.,
The Green, Bradgate Road, Anstey,
Leicester, LE7 7FU, England.
Tel: (00 44) **0116 236 4325**
Fax: (00 44) **0116 234 0205**

THE ADVENTURESS

Ann Barker

Florence Browne lives in poverty with her miserly father, but seeking adventure, she goes to Bath under the assumed name Lady Firenza Le Grey. But there, she meets a man calling himself Sir Vittorio Le Grey, who accuses her of being an adventuress. When her previous suitor, Gilbert Stapleton, visits Bath, Florence is plagued by doubts. Is Sir Vittorio the wicked Italian he appears to be? Are Mr Stapleton's professions of love sincere? And how can she accept an offer of marriage from anyone while she is still living a lie?